KENOPSIA – BOOK 1

UNIVERSITY BOULEVARD

ARAM SAN

Publisher: Inspiring Publishers
P.O. Box 159, Calwell, ACT Australia 2905
http://www.inspiringpublishers.com

A catalogue record for this book is available from the National Library of Australia

National Library of Australia The Prepublication Data Service

Author: Aram San
Title: University Boulevard
Genre: Fiction

Paperback ISBN: 978-1-922792-72-3
Hardcover ISBN: 978-1-922792-73-0
Ebook ISBN: 978-1-922792-74-7

I clenched my fist in grief and punched it in rage.

The mirror shattered into a thousand pieces.

I looked at the trembling faces. "God does not exist... and if it does, it's nothing but a useless dummy," said the broken faces.

And I just stared into their eyes... feeling nothing but a hazy shade of "Kenopsia" inside my fragile world.

CHAPTER 1

(First Year)

I

will never forget that scorching summer. It was late evening when I left her place and sauntered to the university dormitory. Still drowning in her sweet floral scent, I saw how delicately my dream finally flew out of its tarnished cocoon. One of those first moments in life which would never happen again. My life could have been different if I had stayed at her apartment that night.

I met Taban at university. Large, glittering black eyes like a night sky full of stars, long, glowing eyelashes, and wide, thick ruby lips on her round face amplified her alluring charm. Two weeks before I met her for the first time, I was a thousand kilometres away, in my room lying down on the bed, listening to a piece of folklore music, trying to calm myself down. I was still living with my parents in Tehran, the capital city of Iran, a megacity surrounded by a stunning range of mountains on the north side and a chain of historical towns within desert-ish territories in the south.

The university's admission results were supposed to be released via the national government newspapers after two o'clock. Although the admission system was entirely different from other countries in the world, it was quite straightforward. Candidates could select the academic fields and the universities in different cities. They could apply for up to fifty preferences to the Ministry of Education before taking a super competitive nationwide exam. The higher their total points on the exam, the better university they could enter. The result would be announced via governmental newspaper showing accepted candidates' name and the codes associated with the university. My first preferences were all well-known universities in Tehran. I'd also selected several high-ranking universities in different cities just in case I couldn't reach the required point for the colleges in my hometown.

The rhythm and melody of a folk song filled the room, but I was unable to glue them together. It was like scattered words that came into one ear and went out the other ear as my mind was somewhere else. *What if my result isn't good enough to stay here?* was restlessly hovering inside my mind. "No, no I'll get the admission in Tehran. I will stay in my hometown," I whispered, glancing at the clock on the wall near my bookcase. "Oh boy! It's about the time." I tried to stop the shaking in my hands while I put on a pair of jeans and a plain green T-shirt.

The closest magazine kiosk in the neighbourhood to buy newspaper was just a few minutes away, located at the end of a narrow street adjacent to my home. Sneaking out, I tried to escape from the sunlight by dodging my way through the tiny shadows of tall trees and buildings on both sides of the street. A white delivery truck with a colourful image of a smiling cow blocked the narrow street while aiming to park backward near a small grocery store. A burly guy in a black shirt was helping the truck driver to park in the tiny space near the shop.

He shouted, "Left, more left…slowly, slowly…enough. Stop!"

Four or five cars were stuck behind the truck and honked randomly while an old man and three ladies with small shopping baskets stood in the slender pedestrian way staring at the white truck. Apparently, they were in no rush to move and were quite amused by the traffic jam. I shifted a bit and tried to pass them by, walking on the small curb of the tiny water canal between the pedestrian way and the street. A noisy motorcycle raced between the honking cars, leaning right and left, and hit the side mirror of the old, dusty white Renault while trying to overtake the truck.

"Donkey! Are you blind?" the agitated driver inside the Renault yelled at the motorcyclist before adjusting the mirror.

Passing the delivery truck, I glanced at the small yellow kiosk at the end of the street in front of a local mosque with two turquoise minarets where a bunch of young girls and boys formed a short, disordered queue waiting to get their results. Some of them were frequently pacing back and forth, trying to guess their results. I joined the queue near a sweaty, chubby boy with an older man, probably his brother. The boy was gently biting his fingernails and kicking a dry pinecone on the ground while his brother kept looking at his watch.

Twenty minutes had passed when I spotted it. An old motorcycle came cruising around the corner noisily. My heart pounded inside my chest stronger than usual. It wasn't the motorcycle that I cared about, though. It was the pile of newspapers, wrapped in a brown sheet and fastened with an amber ribbon that caught my eye. As soon as the newspapers had been delivered, a brouhaha broke out in the crowd and the line started to creep forward. Trying to avoid contact with others in the sluggish queue, I picked up one newspaper, paid for it with faded coins, and strode back home faster than my usual pace, eager to find out the admission results. The result that would shape my future.

Soundlessly, I entered the apartment, tiptoed to my bedroom, and quickly closed the door. Swift coldness stirred among my fingers and crept to my wrist as I was about to find out my future. My parents had known that the university's admission results were scheduled to be released that day, but they were swamped with their routines. My father owned a construction company, and that was the reason he was usually busy at his office or out of the town on business trips. "My man! I'm sure you'll get what you want. Don't worry about it," said he amicably the other night when my mother told him about my excitement or better to say agitation about the admission outcome. My mother had an engineering degree, but she'd stopped working a long time ago when my oldest and the only brother was born. When I came back home, she was on the phone talking with my grandmother, trying to convince her to have another surgery.

I didn't want to distract them till I was sure I'd gotten accepted. I had a plan to jump out of my room, shout, and surprise my mother, and then call my father and make him happy with the good news. "Let's see." I sighed anxiously, opened the newspaper, and laid it on the handcrafted Persian carpet in front of my bed. My hands trembled slightly over the newspaper. Moving down my index finger on the columns of surnames, I scanned all the names, one after another, until I found mine. It was my name, meaning I got the admission. A waft of relief combined with the joy of success thrilled me, but it didn't last for more than a few seconds. I couldn't believe my eyes. I gazed at my name again and followed the line... same result, no change. I felt my blood pumping to my skull, warming up my whole body. Searching through the results again, I was disappointed to see that nothing had changed. There, in tiny black letters, were the words *Mechanical Engineering*, but that was not my hometown's code listed beside it. It was not what I had expected. It was not what I was hoping for. My eyes were fixed on the wide-open newspaper, but I couldn't see anything.

A knock sounded at the door. "Nima, telephone! It is Farid."

I grabbed the newspaper and folded it up before my mother opened the door and came in. A glance at my face, and she knew that something was wrong.

She raised the receiver to her ear and calmly said, "Nima can't talk now. He'll call you later."

She dropped the wireless receiver on my bed, then sat next to me. "What's that look on your face, big boy? What's happened?" She leaned forward and spotted the semi-crumpled newspaper behind me on the carpet. "Oh, honey. When did you get out? Is this the admission results?"

I grimaced. "Grand State University in Mashhad, not Tehran."

My mother stared back at me. "Mashhad?" Her sympathetic eyes widened behind her brown framed glasses with thick lenses. She paused for a second, then shifted to sit on the ground near me. "This is great! Congratulations. Mashhad is a huge city and has a fantastic academic ranking." She hugged me tight and kissed my cheek and forehead a couple of times. "This is remarkable. Well done, my boy. I'm gonna tell your dad now."

"Mom, didn't you hear me," I whispered. "Mashhad. A different city. I have to move there."

She smiled. "Come on, sweetie. Mashhad is a well-developed city. Moreover, your dad's sisters and brothers are there. You got the engineering admission as you aimed for. This is great! You should be proud of yourself."

I glanced down and realized my hands were not shaking anymore.

She kissed me again, then stood, took the receiver from my bed and called my father. After a moment of speaking, she handed me the phone.

"Nima, well done, man," said my father firmly. "I'm so proud of you. This is such brilliant news. It doesn't matter whether you're in Tehran or Mashhad! It's gonna be a great adventure."

My father's words made me relax. I had not thought about it that way. It was sort of true; this would be far more adventurous!

Seconds after I hung up, the phone rang again.

"Hello?" I answered.

"Did you get the result?" It was my friend, Kian.

"Yes, I did. Mashhad," replied I reluctantly.

"What? You've got to be kidding me? Mashhad?" He shouted.

"Yes. I'm not happy about it at all. I'm confused now. What about you?"

Kian was talking to his parents at the same time and told them about my result. "Tehran," he answered. "Oh boy! This is interesting! So, you and Farid will be together. Lucky, you two!"

"What?"

"Hasn't he told you about his result? He's been accepted by Mashhad Grand State University, too."

"You don't say! Seriously? I'm gonna call him now."

Mixed feelings jiggled my arms and soon transformed into a short puff followed by a weird smile on my face. I immediately called Farid and it turned out we had both been accepted to the same university, same college, and the very same engineering field; a coincidence that would change our lives forever and shape our destinies.

II

Almost two weeks later, at the end of September, I said goodbye to my mother, left my home, and realized my teenage years were over. Moving out of my parents' home filled me with a bizarre mood, my first taste of independence, maybe. A new start? Not only was I leaving my safe haven, but I was also about to commence an undeniably new period of my life. The prospect of living far from my parents, in another city, and with different people virtually blew up my mind. Appreciating every last moment before I became a true adult, I warmly embraced my mother and kissed her while trying to keep my emotions in check. On the other side, my mother had always shown strength when dealing with emotional situations. She never cried, or if she did, I never knew about it. "You'll be fine. We'll be visiting you often. Love you," were her kind words trailed by a warm tight hug and goodbye kisses.

I was about to burst into tears when my father yelled, "Alright, that's enough. Come on, big boy. Farid and his dad are here. Time to go."

I kissed my mother again and dragged my suitcase out of my parents' home.

Four hours later, we were stepping up into our train cabin, an old, four-bed compartment with a tiny TV and two small sliding side tables near a scratched-up window behind a thick faded dark green curtain. A fourteen-hour trip was in front of us, but that wasn't my concern at all.

It was fortunate that Farid and I could be together during the journey. Our fathers kept chatting, laughing, and looking for common memories from their past years. They occasionally pulled our legs and tried to cheer us up by singing famous old songs, telling stories from their time at university, or giving tips about relationships.

"This is going to be the best period of your life, boys. I still remember those days when I sneaked out of my classes to meet your mom. Oh, man!" said my father excitedly.

"And where did you two meet?" grinned Farid's father, winking at me.

I smiled without engaging myself as my head was occupied with thousands of questions. The change was enormous, and it all happened unbelievably fast. On one hand, I was upset about leaving my parents, my friends, my city, and my home;

but on the other hand, I was excited to start a fresh chapter, learn about another city, find new friends, make independent decisions, and live a new life.

It was getting late, and we decided to sleep. I chose the upper bed, waited for a bit till the train passed a long curving path, and stopped shaking. I jumped up to my bunk without stepping on the small ladder attached to the bedside while my father opened the upper section of the cabin's window to get some fresh air. The squealing sound of the train wheels mixed with the uproar of thundering wind, filling the room. Farid was on the other upper bed opposite mine. Glimpsing at him, I pulled the thick curtain back and glanced out. I couldn't see anything but the shining sky. The window was covered in scratches, but the sky was amazingly beautiful, clear and full of stars. It looked like we were in the heart of the desert. I closed the curtain again and tried to sleep by laying my head on the tiny, hard pillow.

Listening to the rhythmic rumbling sounds of the railway tracks, I closed my eyes and my brain switched to dream mode, where I found myself in the first year of intermediate school. It was the break time between two classes. A group of pupils, all boys, were happily singing in the small schoolyard. I was playing football with my classmates on the other side of the yard. I kicked the ball, targeting to score a goal, but the ball rolled into the underground parking area near the schoolyard. I ran and passed the ramp to the parking lot. It was almost empty of cars but filled with heaps of postal boxes in different sizes. Carelessly looking for the red and white striped plastic ball, I caught a glimpse of a shadow. He was one of my classmates, appeared from behind the boxes. I recognized him very well. He used to sit near me in our class. He had grey eyes, wearing a blue sweater with a high neck collar. I forgot why I was there as he took his steps toward me. The underground garage miraculously turned into our classroom on the second floor of the school building. I was standing near the door; my hands were on his back caressing the soft skin under the warmth of his sweater, while his arms were flung around my shoulders. I gently moved my right hand towards his neck and touched his lips with the tips of my fingers. My left hand slowly moved up and down on his spine. He stared at me silently with wide-open eyes as I pressed my right leg between his and kissed him on the lips smoothly. We could hear our heartbeats; it was hot, and we were sweating together. Our bodies warmly merged as I took his sweater off and moved my hand down to his velvety pants. Rubbing his soft thigh, I heard someone knocking on the classroom door, shouting, "Pray time! Pray time!" I was out of breath. He started to shiver, and I tried to run, but could not take a single step.

"Pray time! Pray time!"

The punitive loud voice echoed, and someone was continuously knocking on the door. Suddenly, a man with an ugly face covered in curly, black beard opened the door. I was frightened and unable to move. He stretched his arms towards me, and… I woke up in sweaty underwear.

It took a few seconds till I remembered where I was. Inside of our cabin was quite hot and stuffy. I glanced out; the sky was still dark with a few stars.

"Where are we?" I asked under my breath.

"Not a clue! Sleep," Farid replied with broken words.

We were at a train station in the middle of nowhere. The train crews were shouting, "Pray time! Pray time!" They knocked on all the cabin doors to wake up the passengers for morning prayer in an old, dirty mosque at that train station. It was part of the train crew's duty to knock on each cabin's door, informing passengers that the train stopped, and it was the time for prayer in the morning. They kept shouting, "Pray time! Pray time!"

III

It was about ten in the morning when we arrived in the city that would totally transform my life. As we left the central train station, a smooth ray of warmth from the half-cloudy sky pushed my eyelids down and a chilled breeze tingled my ears, announcing that autumn was on its way. Most of the passengers hurriedly dragged their suitcases to the exit gate, while the public speaker repeatedly announced departing train schedules. We took a cab from the train station taxi service and headed to my aunt's place.

My father was in the front seat chitchatting with the young driver, mainly about changes in the city during the last eighteen years. A strong but pleasant wind slapped my face randomly while I looked out of the half-opened window and thought about the place where I would spend the next chapter of my life. The city wasn't new to me as my family used to travel there often, so I remembered some streets and different areas when the cab reached downtown.

Farid was talking with his father about opening a bank account. He turned his head to me. "Nima, what time is the university enrolment? Two or four in the afternoon?"

I thought for a second before answering, "Um, we have to be there at two o'clock for the orientation, and then enrolment will start at four."

Farid looked back at his father. "Today is Wednesday. We are busy with enrolment the whole day and can't finish everything by Friday. You should stay here longer."

I knew what Farid was worried about. We had decided to rent an apartment and share it together. Neither I nor Farid were keen on residing in the university dormitory. The plan was to arrive on Wednesday, sort out the enrolment, and then look for a flat to rent. If we had enough time, we could buy some essential housewares before our fathers left us. They couldn't stay for more than a few days. My father had asked his brother to find somewhere suitable for us almost a week ago. This would help us save lots of time. We were talking about our plan and how to finish everything in less than three days when the cab turned left into an alley with a round impasse at the end.

This was where my aunt's family lived. It was a small, quiet alley with thick, old plane trees on both sides. I knew my aunt's home very well—an old, three-story building in an expensive area of the town with one unit on each floor. Her apartment was on the second floor. My grandparents used to live there. I was looking at the trees with almost dried amber-colour leaves in front of the building when I saw my uncle waving his hand at us from the entrance.

Greeting everybody, he helped us bring our suitcases upstairs. My aunts were happily standing in front of the rustic wooden door, loudly welcoming us. Done with the kisses and hugs, we sat on the classical-style armchairs in the enormous living room. The guest salon floor was covered with two vast, silk Persian carpets and packed with different types of green plants in big clay vases near the enormous window. I knew the name of dieffenbachia, but was clueless about the others. By lunchtime, my father's family were all gathered to welcome us as part of our tradition. I had two uncles and two aunts, all younger than my father. They were married and each had two children. My grandparents had passed away about ten years ago, both in the same year. Since then, my oldest aunt's family had been living in that huge apartment.

Question after question, suggestion after suggestion were hitting Farid and I non-stop. I had never felt that close to my father's family, maybe because I was always living in a different city far from them. Finally, my aunt called, "Lunch is ready. Please, come around the table and help yourselves."

I stared at Farid after we had our meal, and he nodded his head like he read my mind.

"Um, thanks for the lunch. It was so delicious." I repeated it a few times to my aunt and glanced at Farid again. "Um, we must go now."

Farid smiled and followed my lead before another round of questions began. Farid was a handsome boy, always cautious about his attire, and tried to dress smart. We knew each other for about six years. He had a muscular chest with strong shoulders, brown eyes, and short black hair. His white teeth and trimmed eyebrows combined with his charm attracted many girls. He was, however, completely unfamiliar with the city.

We passed three alleys and rambled towards the city's famous street, Shahid Boulevard. Both sides of the street were shaded by different types of trees. Dried orange leaves crumbled under pedestrians' footsteps on the pavement while faded green leaves were experiencing the last moments of their lives.

"I love autumn. So beautiful," I whispered.

"What?" Farid asked.

"Isn't it beautiful? Autumn?"

"Um, it is."

We both were quieter than usual. Looking around, Farid asked me, "How many times we can get back home during each semester?"

"Um… No idea!" I answered with hesitation.

We finally arrived on Shahid Boulevard.

"This area is the city's hot spot," I told Farid.

"Looks pretty. How much does it cost to rent a unit here?"

"Beats me! Shouldn't be cheap. Hope we find a nice one soon."

My younger uncle had a friend in real estate who was chasing a flat for us. Due to old traditions and cultural beliefs, renting a place for young singles was preposterously difficult in Iran, particularly in religious cities, and Mashhad was one such place. That was why our fathers needed to stay with us to rent a flat. They had to assure the landlord that we would behave, prove we had families, and promise we wouldn't create trouble—meaning no girls, no alcohol, no smoking, and in some cases, even no music! Wandering along Shahid Boulevard, we faced the very first moments of our new life as an enormous park packed with trees at the end of the Boulevard caught our eye.

"That should be a fine place for jogging. What's it called?" Farid asked me quietly.

"Azad Park. Yes, not bad. It has a track for running and some pitches for badminton, as far as I remember!"

The park was famous for different reasons, from the vast playground for kids and picturesque gardens, to frequent pickpocketing and notorious drug dealing points at night. My aunt had told us the university was located in front of the park's central gate.

"Let's go up there," I told Farid, and we headed up to the pedestrian bridge over a busy road that linked Shahid Boulevard to the park. We stopped on the bridge and scanned the panoramic view same as many other people who were crossing the street via the bridge. Cars crossed underneath the bridge, disappearing on the opposite side, toward the mountains. A huge wheel with colourful cabins rose amongst amber and greenish trees in the centre of the park's playground. On the opposite side, Shahid Boulevard was visible from one end to the other with all the shops, traffic lights, and parallel trees on both sides of the street.

"Man, this is astonishing. Look! That should be our university!" Farid said and pointed to the mountain side.

"Yes, it is. I read it somewhere that the complex is massive. Oh boy! Look at that," I paused. "A town inside another city!"

It took almost an hour to find the Engineering Department, located in a giant, five-story building with a yellow perforated brick façade.

"Lucky we got out of my aunt's place early," I told Farid when we reached the college. The university campus was a giant compound that included dormitories, restaurants, an amphitheatre, cafés, a football pitch, and, of course, various academic and administration buildings. The university's bus services were available to transfer students and staff from the central entrance to the dormitories, from restaurants to colleges, from the amphitheatre to the west gate, and so on.

"What time is it?" I asked Farid.

He glanced at his watch. "A quarter to two. Better rush!"

We eventually found our way to the area designated for new students. We haven't seen an information desk, but spotted a man with a short beard who was guiding the others near the tiny welcome sign.

Approaching him, I glanced at the other students. Girls were mostly in black or grey Islamic outfits, while boys wore a bit more colourful clothes. I was in light-blue jeans with a striped blue and white long-sleeved shirt, while Farid had put on bright grey jeans and a plain white long-sleeved shirt. I had a hunch that our outfits were quite different from those of the other guys.

"Excuse me? Hello! We're looking for the orientation session for new students. The program shows it starts at two in front of the Engineering College," I said to the man with a short beard.

"Right there." He pointed at a group of other students thirty metres away from the gate near the college's café. I glanced at Farid. "Let's go!" We walked there, joining the new students who were hanging around, waiting for someone to announce something. I was excited, looking around without any purpose, until I saw her.

It was the first time I saw Taban. Her vibrant black eyes were like an unexplored constellation on the celestial sphere of night. She was talking with other girls while waiting for the orientation to start. For a split second, our glances tangled together. It was a peculiar moment as I almost forgot how to exhale, and then she smiled.

IV

The last glow of the sun was about to set when we returned to my aunt's apartment. We quickly replied to our fathers' question about our first impressions of the university, and hastily wrapped up our story about how the orientation had gone. Both of us, Farid and I, had the same thing in our heads.

"Have you had a chance to find a place for us?" was my question to my uncle which came out in haste but politely.

"Huh, someone has no patience," chuckled my uncle. He added, "Not many options are available in the market. I'm waiting till tomorrow as my friend told me about a perfect opportunity to rent a proper flat for you, guys. I've already set up a quick visit for tomorrow morning." He stared at me and Farid, paused for a second, and then explained more about the real estate business in the city. "My friend found some places, but they were all like rat holes. You know," he paused and turned down his voice like he was about to tell us a secret. "No one is willing to rent out their apartment to singles—specifically, students. It is very problematic to find an appropriate place. But," he raised his voice suddenly, "my friend had a long chat with one of his clients and convinced the landlord that you two young men are different." His voice turned back to a normal tone as he continued, "Your families are well-known, and you are from Tehran—you know! From the capital city."

The next day, we visited the place. It was a small, two-bedroom underground apartment not far from our university with a tiny kitchen and a stained bathroom. The flat had only one narrow, opaque window with no handle to open it because it faced directly to the street pedestrian way.

My uncle's friend, the chatterbox real estate agent, said, "This is the best you can find in town. I had a long discussion with the owner and finally convinced him. He doesn't lease this apartment to single students, you know."

I stared at the half-empty bedrooms and the corner of my mouth moved down in disappointment.

"Does it have a telephone landline?" Farid asked.

"Oh, no. You can't find a landline for underground apartments, buddy. But you may buy it yourself later," the real estate agent answered without showing any interest in the question. "The walls are painted recently, the kitchen has a gas stovetop, and most importantly, you have a washing machine. Believe me, none of the other underground places are equipped with a washing machine. What else do you want? This is a perfect fit for you two young men."

It was a total bummer for us. The agent kept talking while I glanced at Farid and whispered, "This is terrible! But we don't have any other choice for now."

"Awful! I don't know."

"What should we do? Our dads are leaving tomorrow, and the landlord will only make a deal with them, not us. He's only letting us rent this shithole under our dads' names, with their signatures. No one deals with single students. This is so stupid!"

Our fathers signed the contract that evening and left back to Tehran the day after. The night we moved in was a bit weird for both of us. Neither I nor Farid were in the mood to chat. It was like a hurricane of mixed emotions inside my head trying to release, but a thick lock bolted on my mouth, holding my thoughts from storming out. We quietly headed to our rooms and pretended that we were sleeping.

Lying down on a small wooden bed against the wall, I tried to sleep for almost an hour, but random thoughts kept me awake. On one hand, leaving my family and starting a new life in a stinky, underground unit without any real window simulated a gloomy dungeon atmosphere, but on the other hand, it was a moving but strange inspiration to experience an independent life. I was picturing the university, classrooms, laboratories, libraries full of people who were hanging around. Sitting with girls in the same classroom for the first time in my life was indeed something unusual and exhilarating for me, as mixed-gender schools were not allowed in Iran. I took a deep breath and tried to sleep, but then my childhood memories kept me awake. I struggled not to think about why boys and girls had to study in separate schools by shutting my eyes, laying my folded arms over my forehead and picturing the charming girl who smiled at me at the beginning of the orientation session.

CHAPTER 2

I

was out of breath. My eyes were burning while a sharp, bitter dryness in my throat was amplifying the intense pain in my back. I limped to the tiny window, hardly keeping my balance as I was blindsided, frightened, and shocked. A bit disoriented, I sat on the cold ground tiles in the men's toilet room. The more I tried to figure out the situation, the less I could understand as there was no time to think. We had to get out of that hell.

A few minutes later I heard no more screaming as harsh squashing sounds and patchy breaking noises almost faded out. I put both hands over my eyes and tried to calm down the piercing pain. "How the fuck can we escape from the building" was my only thought while gently pushing my spine into the wall and stretching my left leg, hoping to relieve the ache in my back. I couldn't open my right eye and the left one was still burning.

I was about to lose consciousness but managed to stay a bit focused, breathe normally and listen to my surroundings until running tap water and faint cracking sounds caught my attention.

For just a few moments, I'd forgotten where I was, and I suddenly remembered the first day of university, and Taban.

II

It was a quarter past seven in the morning when the loud, intermittent alarm from a small cubical clock on the bedside table went off. It wasn't the darkness of the room or the warmth of a fluffy blanket around me that made me want to stay in bed. I couldn't keep my eyes shut as a howling of excitement inside my head didn't slow down the night before. Turning from one side to another, I listened to scattered noises from the kitchen. Something like cracking glasses and plates under running tap water. I managed to get up and turn on the light while I was thinking, *today could be the first day of many things, the start of thrilling events in my life. I'm going to make a change in the world!*

Yawning, I pushed the door open, and said, "Good morning, roomie. What are you doing, pal?"

Farid was busy washing a rusted kettle to make tea.

"Forget about it. Let's go! It is the first day at uni! We'll have our breakfast in that cosy café near the college," I suggested with half-opened eyes, then tried to find my way to the toilet.

"Good idea. Let's get out of here! I can't take the rust out of this bloody kettle!" Farid responded without hesitation, wiping his hands with a dish towel.

A little while later, dressed in smart casual, we took our backpacks and eagerly headed out.

Our place was in a tiny, quiet alley not far from Abad Boulevard, which was the most common way to the university. We could take a cab or simply walk.

"Let's take a walk, buddy! It is a nice warm day!" I asked Farid as we turned onto Abad Boulevard. The street was famous for having a series of old, tall green trees, mostly plain trees, on both sides. They formed an endless, green semi-tunnel on top of the street with flying sparrows and spotted doves around. It was like a natural air pumping station for the entire city. Wandering under the long-lasting shadow was refreshing on hot summer days. In the middle of the street was a short column of well-trimmed green boxwood with designated openings in between to cross the boulevard from one side to the other.

Walking along the street under the morning shadow of tall trees, we reached the university in less than forty minutes and walked to the Engineering College. It looked different in comparison to the orientation day last week. The parking lot near the college was packed with cars, and many students were hanging out in the college's café or outdoor yard opposite the primary gate. Our first course was going to start at ten in the morning, and we had almost an hour to burn. The café wasn't a real building made from cement or bricks. It was an enclosure with a massive bamboo structure that was covered with olive green tarpaulin fabric like a giant tent.

Entering the café, I looked for a free table. All the wooden tables were alike, not new, slightly scratched-up, the same size with enough seats for six to eight people. The sides of the café were protected by a thick, transparent plastic sheet, like an enormous greenhouse, and it had two separate entrances, one for women, and the other for men. It was one of those enigmatic Islamic rules in Iran to separate women from men as much as possible. The kitchen was in the centre, completely isolating the men's section from the women's area. From time to time, I could overhear random conversations from both sides. I guessed most of them were senior students who were reunited after the summer holiday. In the men's section, they were staring at us in such a way that made me feel like we were passing through airport security.

"What's our classroom number?" asked Farid while we were having our breakfast.

I took out the semester schedule from my backpack and scanned it. "Um, let's see. General Chemistry-1, classroom number two-oh-five."

We finished our breakfast and left, entering the college building from the second entrance, a quite small double-gated door, which was near the café at the south end of the building.

"The first digit of each room indicates the floor," I told Farid as we headed to the second level. Students were everywhere in the corridor, heading in random ways, creating an indecipherable humming sound. A group of boys slowed down in front of us and suddenly disappeared into a tiny door on the right-hand side of the walkway while at the same time a bunch of girls sluggishly passed us, talking together in low pitch. Some students had had their first class at eight o'clock, and it seemed like the rest were wandering around the building or looking for their classrooms.

I was eyeing around when Farid poked me. "Hey, where are you going?" He was pointing to a small signboard on the wall, saying, "*Hello!* Room two-oh-five, buddy!" We stopped in front of the grey double doors, each with a small rectangular window to see what was happening inside. Glancing at Farid, I opened the door and entered a spacious room with eighty wooden chairs, bolted to the floor in two sections. Large windows on the left side generously brought the daylight into the classroom, where a white podium for professors and two green chalkboards covered almost the entire front wall.

Stepping into the room, I spotted three guys sitting at the end of the room in the right section. One of them was a bit hefty with a brown sweater. A girl in a black chador, a full body cloak, had already taken a seat in the left section. I could only see her pale brown face. Chador was an outer garment that completely covered a woman's head and body, except the face. It was like a full-length semi-circle fabric that comes down to the ground without any slits or pocket for hands.

"Hello," I said loudly across the room. "Is this the General Chemistry-1 tutorial?"

"Hi. Yes, it is," replied one of the guys at the end of the classroom.

Farid and I approached the boys, shook hands, and said nothing to the girl as she pretended not to see or hear us.

Looking around, I asked Farid, "Where should we put our butts, buddy?"

He pointed to the third row. "Let's sit there!"

Other students—both boys and girls—came in alone or in small groups during the next five or ten minutes. Girls sat in the left section of the room and boys in the right. Some of them formed a tiny colony by sitting near each other and chatting quietly. Evidently, they knew each other.

"How disappointing. Where are the hot chicks?" I asked Farid under my breath.

"Hope some beautiful girls join our classroom this semester or I will quit," Farid whispered and smiled.

Most of the girls were wearing black chadors. Some other girls wore casual hijab outfit which was like a full-length, robe-like outer garment that covered the whole body except the head, feet and hands. They covered heads with khimar, which was like a wide cape, covering their hair, neck, and shoulders. The more casual hijab, a scarf to cover their head and neck, was not allowed at the university. They must wear either a chador or a full-length outer garment with a khimar. Most of the girls ignored the boys as they entered the room. I glanced around. The boys were talking amongst themselves, and the girls were chatting together.

A few minutes later, I bent to take my brand-new hardcover lab notebook out of my backpack when I heard a soft voice from behind me.

"Hello!"

I swiftly turned to the left and there she was, the charming girl with large sparkling eyes from the orientation day. I remembered her on the spot. Keeping her smile, she sat near me but in the left section of the classroom.

"Hello," I muttered as my muscles stopped moving for a couple of seconds.

"We saw each other in the orientation," she said. "I didn't realize that we'd be in the same class."

This felt like one of those moments in life which would never be repeated. It was like I had accidentally passed a curtain of fire.

I foolishly answered, "Yes. Very good," and stupidly turned back and pretended to search for something in my backpack. My hands trembled a bit inside my backpack while my heart began to beat faster inside my chest. Gathering all my courage, I turned back to apologize, introduce myself and talk more with her, but it was too late as she was chatting with other girls.

A few minutes later, the professor entered the classroom, and it was how our first course had formally started.

Less than two hours later, when our first course was finished and the professor had left the class, Farid turned to me.

"Not a single catch. I hope new ladies join our classes before the graduation ceremony." He winked and whispered in my ear, "That one, fifth row near the window seems cute, and the girl beside you."

Farid continued copying whatever the professor had written on the chalkboard while I glanced at the charming girl near me and turned back to Farid.

"She doesn't wear a chador. Her attire shows she isn't one of those religious fanatics. She also talked to me when she entered the classroom, which was kind of surprising."

Farid grinned and replied, "Oh, yes, I got that."

We put our stuff in our backpacks and looked around the half-full room. I counted; there were only twenty-eight students. The girls were talking together, louder than the boys. A small group of them seemed to get along quickly, including the charming girl who had sat next to me, and I did not know her name yet.

"I'm Farid, and he's my friend, Nima." I turned back. Farid was speaking with three other boys on the other side of the room almost near the door. I waved my hand, grabbed my backpack, and joined them.

"Hi, I'm Nima. How's it going?"

They introduced themselves politely—Abbas, Reza, Kami.

"Where are you from?" I asked them with a friendly tone.

"I'm from Tehran," Abbas answered.

"Me, too," Kami replied in a low tone.

"I'm from Sari," Reza responded. His grey eyes narrowed a bit as sunlight landed on his face. I noticed that he pronounced "R" from the back of his throat like the French.

"So, you guys are all together? How do you know each other?" Farid asked while we left the class altogether.

"We're living on the same floor in the dormitory. Actually, I and Reza are roommates," Abbas answered. He was the muscular boy in a brown sweater whom I had seen when I entered the class that morning, but we did not have a chance to get along more. He was taller than the others with a sharp nose and long chin.

We stood in the hallway waiting for the next class, which was about to kick off in the adjacent room.

"What about you two?" Abbas asked us.

"We're from Tehran, too. We're pals since our first year of high school," I answered and simultaneously pushed the doorknob.

"Get in, everybody! Welcome to the second tutorial of uni!" I shouted and stood aside like a doorman to let the others get in first.

A blink of surprise appeared on everyone's look except Farid. They had not expected me to act like that, but after a short moment, they got the joke and burst out with laughter.

"He's always like that," explained Farid coolly.

A quick glance around the room was enough to realize that this class consisted of almost the same classmates from the previous course, sitting in similar spots.

"Hi, everybody!" I said excitedly and followed Farid. No "hi" back from the girls again.

The charming girl with the huge, twinkling eyes was sitting in the same seat as in the last tutorial, staring at me. I couldn't avoid a sudden smile on my face as a delightful sense of familiarity swirled inside my chest, pushing me towards her. This time, I didn't ask Farid where to sit and choose the same spot without hesitation as I wanted to somehow redeem myself from the stupid shyness that I showed in the previous class.

"Farid, let's sit here," I murmured in his ear and dropped my backpack down on the front seat.

"Hi," I said quietly to the charming girl.

"Good day again!" she answered firmly with a smile, her white teeth sparkling.

"Do we have Mathematics-1 now?" I asked her with a straight face.

"Yes, we certainly do! Don't you know which course you are attending?" she asked me with a smile, her right eyebrow lifting up a bit.

"Um, not really. I'm just following my friend. I go wherever he goes!" I pointed to Farid and then both of us chuckled. It was such a pleasant moment for me. I was about to ask her name and introduce myself, but the Mathematics professor entered the class and a sudden silence shut me down. He began the course by reading students' names and checking the attendance sheet. I was all ears to figure out the charming girl's name. Other classmates were also keen to figure out each other's identities. I glanced back and noted everyone carefully looking at the professor's mouth, chasing each name. Girls were subtly looking at their right in an effort not to raise attention, and boys were turning left secretly.

"Miss Taban Pakzad?" asked the professor, and she raised her hand.

"Taban Pakzad." I repeated it under my breath, glancing at her.

The course finished a bit early, and we didn't have any more classes for the rest of the day. Guys were asking each other to have lunch in the central canteen while girls were talking at the other corner of the room near the window.

"What do you think?" Farid asked me. "Should we go back to our place, or join them for lunch?"

"Let's stay here a bit longer" was my affirmative reply without any need to think.

I hesitantly glimpsed at Taban, hoping to get her attention. She eyed me back like she felt my gaze, and gently nodded her head, smiling.

I left the class with the other boys and headed downstairs to the main corridor. A group of three or four guys were talking in the passageway, and a tiny girl with a bunch of papers in her hands walked into one of the nearby rooms and disappeared. We stuck together like a group of tourists and followed our tour guide, Abbas, who explained in a low tone what else was happening at the university besides our semester courses.

"This is the Student's Cultural Unit, and this one is the Student's Islamic Association called the Basij Organization." Abbas showed us two doors opposite each other, almost in the middle of the corridor.

The Basij Organization's door was closed. Getting closer to the Cultural Unit, I overheard voices, so I stuck my head in for a second. A few boys and girls were around a rectangular wooden table, talking together. A couple of metres farther, Abbas pointed to the right side of the corridor and said, "This is the Student's Science Committee." An A4-size flyer was attached to the door: "Welcome to the new academic year..."

"Nima, come on," Farid called. "What are you doing there?"

He was standing with the other boys in the main hall at the end of the corridor, a round area just before the building's front entrance. The side walls were all covered by various announcement boards that belonged to different student's associations.

"How the hell do you know all these rooms and associations?" I asked Abbas.

"Huh, not all of them. We came here with other folks from the dormitory last week. They had been here for some years and knew everything. They showed us around, and briefly explained different student organizations and how they function."

We walked out of the building, continuing our tour towards the canteen.

"There are different paths to the canteen," Reza said this time, and chose the most popular way, University Boulevard, a two-way avenue with a spacious sidewalk path for pedestrians. A narrow water canal separated the pavement from the street. "This is the Faculty of Science." Reza pointed to the right side of the street at three blocks that were attached together and formed a gigantic white building. We turned to the right, passed a bus station, and I recognized the amphitheatre building a bit farther near the grass-covered football pitch. "This area belongs to the Sports College," Abbas explained and showed us another white one-story building. "There we go. This is the uni restaurant," he shouted happily as we approached the entry. The canteen was also divided into two isolated sections separating men from women. Walking towards the building, my eyes fixed on sign boards on top of each door that read: *Brother's Entrance* and *Sister's Entrance*. It was another way of calling men and women in Iran, mostly amongst religious people.

I picked a metallic platter from a rack of trays near the doorway as we entered the canteen, and then followed the others to a long queue. Students and some of the university staff were sitting behind a series of long, parallel tables which occupied most of that huge salon. Non-stop clanking noises and vague, scattering chitchats, mixed with the tangy, steamy atmosphere echoed around the entire salon, creating a uniform humming orchestra. Holding the tray, I glanced around and tried to find my lunch coupon inside my jeans' pockets. A chubby guy behind me was talking with his buddy about the high cost of bus tickets or something like that. A group of four men left the salon while talking loudly about a TV show that was on last night. Another man with grey hair—probably university staff—was sitting at the first table near the kitchen, struggling with a toothpick in his mouth.

"The queue of differences!" I said to myself.

"What?" Farid asked me.

"Nothing," I answered while finally taking out the lunch coupon from my pocket.

After lunch, we walked back to our underground apartment, and the other guys headed to the dormitory.

"The first day of the university is finished. Three years and three hundred fifty-one days more to go!" Farid shouted on our way back.

"Not bad, is it?" I answered, chuckling.

"Not bad at all! Oh, Nima, I have to phone my dad and sister."

"Don't you want to wait till the evening when we go to my aunt's home for dinner? You can call them from there."

"Negative. I'd rather call now. It is my sister's birthday today. I must call her now. You go ahead and I'll join you later."

"As you wish! Tell her happy birthday for me, please."

There was a small telephone centre at the end of Shahid Boulevard, and he would have to walk half an hour more to get there. Farid left me alone to think about the last six hours of my life. My mind was so busy with various questions. *Oh, boy. How long is it gonna take till I know everything and everybody? Who are these people? What should I do? What should I not do?*

III

A few days later, an announcement on the Cultural Unit's board in the main hall of the college caught my attention. "A warm welcome to all the students. The opening session will be held at the amphitheatre on Thursday at four o'clock." I adjusted my backpack and thought, *what does it mean? What opening session?*

I had half an hour till my next class, so I turned back to the corridor and headed to the Cultural Unit. The door was half-open, and two boys and a girl were sitting behind a table.

The first thing I noted was a photo of Mosaddegh. He had been one of Iran's prime ministers before the Islamic Revolution. He had successfully led the nationalization of the oil and gas industries at the time. It was bizarre to see his picture on the wall of the Cultural Unit because he was more the nationalist political icon rather than a cultural face.

"Hello. Can I help you?" asked a slim guy with a sharp chin and a meticulously trimmed short box beard. He had a slight hunch on his back, but he was holding his head straight up.

"Hi. Um… I just wanted to ask about the announcement on your board. The one about the opening session?"

"Oh, Karim isn't here now. He's handling the session and has more info about it. By the way, my name is Ali. Nice to meet you."

"Nice to meet you, too. I'm Nima," I responded, and we shook hands.

I glanced at the other guy and shook his hand, too. "I'm Saber," he introduced himself with a friendly smile. He was a quite chubby man with broad shoulders which gave him a unique rectangular-shaped upper body. He was clean-shaven with a round, acne-marked face and narrow eyes. I couldn't see the girl in the room, anymore. Apparently, she had left while we were talking.

"Beginner?" asked Ali.

"Sorry?" I was baffled a bit. "Oh! Yes, just started this week."

Beginner was the title for new students who had just begun university — like a freshman. During the last few days, I learned that students were classified under two categories: their academic field and their year of admission to the university.

"What about you two?" I asked.

"Mechanical engineering, ninety-five."

"Cool! I'm studying mechanical engineering," I answered shortly, and then excused myself. "Thanks, guys. I have to head off to my next class now. It starts in ten minutes."

"No problem. By the way, the opening session is about getting together, finding out about each other, and chatting about cultural activities. There will be music, poetry, drawing, and literature," Ali explained, fast walking with me towards the door.

"Sounds great. I'd love to participate."

"Very well, glad to hear that."

Came the Thursday soon and I joined the session to see what was going on.

"Hi, my name is Nima. I read your advertisement on the board," I said to a smiling, plump guy who was speaking with other students in the amphitheatre, answering their questions, and guiding them to different seats.

"Hello! Nice to meet you. I'm Karim. Ali told me about you the other day," he answered amicably, then led me to a free spot near himself. I was a bit surprised that Ali had told him about my visit to the Cultural Unit.

My eyes moved everywhere like I was in a museum, scanning the students who were sitting on the stage of the amphitheatre in a semi-circle line. Each one had something in front of them, musical instruments, paintings, or books. *Isn't it a bit weird that I have nothing but my backpack? Maybe it's better to leave and come back later?* I thought while pushing the questions away from my head.

Karim kicked off the session and explained a series of activities that we could carry out under the Unit's support. It was a quick introduction, as most of the students were not beginners. Karim waved his hand and pointed to the attendees with his fat index finger, asking them to introduce themselves one by one from left to right. We followed his directions and briefly talked about ourselves.

A well-dressed boy from a northern city played "Asturias" on guitar. His fingers smoothly danced up and down on the fretboard. I closed my eyes for a moment and leaned back in my chair till he finished the piece.

After that, a tall, slim girl in casual hijab with a dark blue khimar showed us her painting on canvas, two birds sitting on a long, curvy electrical cord between two ruined buildings under a grey, smoky sky. I moved closer to see the drawing better as she was explaining her work of art. It was something like a post-war scene. I nodded my head, smiled, but didn't comment or ask anything.

Another guy discussed a recent theatre performance in the city and updated us about the latest news on blockbuster movies. I truly enjoyed the atmosphere. It was a place to talk about everything I liked and get familiar with other opinions. It was an open gate to a different world, and then another door opened, and then the next door...

"I'm interested in literature. Also, I play a couple of traditional Iranian musical instruments—the santur and the daf," I said when it was my turn.

"Amazing. Do you have your musical instrument with you?" asked Karim.

"I brought them from Tehran, and they are at my apartment. Sorry, I didn't know that I should bring them today."

Everybody turned to stare at me.

"You aren't staying in the dorm?" Karim asked, his eyes widening a bit.

"No, I rented an apartment with my friend."

"Wow, great! Ladies and gentlemen, we have an aristocrat beginner in our group!" he shouted, and we all chuckled.

At the end of the meeting, Karim gave us a form to fill in our names, interests, and any suggestions we had. "Oh, book club?" said Karim and nodded when I handed the questionnaire back to him.

"Um, yes. I think it would be interesting to sit around and talk about…"

Karim politely cut my sentence and said, "Absolutely, yes, yes. We do have such sessions, but now, it's time to go."

We picked up our belongings and left the salon in small groups of two or three.

"Do you have time? Let's walk to the Cultural Unit together if you are free," Karim asked me calmly.

"Oh, sure. I have nothing to do."

The rumbling wind blew through the trees as we strolled along the University Boulevard. The sun was about to set, and the sky was gradually changing its colour. It was almost late, and all classes had been finished. The weekend was about to start and not many students were around.

"So, did you start in ninety-five, too? Same as Ali and Saber?" I asked Karim.

"Yes. I've been here for three years. I was supposed to graduate at the end of this year, but huh," he scratched his neck and finished his sentence. "Not a chance." I figured out from his accent that he was from Isfahan, a magnificent historical city in the centre of Iran. Chatting about ourselves to get along more, we arrived at the Cultural Unit. The door was closed, so I assumed no one would be there. Karim opened it without knocking and we entered.

"Oh, hello, you guys. How are you?" Ali greeted us with a smile. A slight hunch on his back magnified his sharp chin under his beard.

Two other young men sat around the table. I recognized Saber, but the other one was new to me.

"Hi, everybody," I said, and we shook hands.

"You met Saber the other day. And this is Jalal," Ali introduced.

Jalal had a large mouth and big eyes that certainly dominated other elements on his face. He came from Bojnord, a small city near Mashhad, and had started civil engineering two years ago.

Saber was drinking tea from a takeaway cup. "Do you want some?"

"No, I'm good. Thanks."

"So, how was the opening session?" Ali asked Karim.

"It went pretty well. The same folks showed up as usual. Some new faces, too. Nima was one of them." He winked at me and continued, "Did you know he plays traditional music?"

Ali raised his eyebrow and said, "Interesting! We can organize a concert, then?"

I wasn't sure if he was joking or not. I cautiously smiled and answered, "Maybe for my graduation."

Karim pulled a chair, glanced at Saber and said, "Nima also suggested a book club."

"Splendid. I'd like that energy!"

Saber was the head of the Cultural Unit. He told me that Ali had been the leader of the Unit two years ago. "He is too old to run the team now," Saber said without any hint of joking. But he couldn't hold his straight face; he glanced at Ali and burst into a peal of laughter.

"Oh, shut up, Saber. I wanted you to do something useful at this college. So, I let you lead the Unit."

We all chuckled.

"So, guys, what were you discussing before we arrived?" Karim asked the group.

"We were talking about a new political movement at Tehran University, an anti-government protest. Anyway, we'll talk later," Ali answered briefly, crossing his arms. "Do you know there are several elections at the university every year?" He glanced at me and didn't wait for a response. "Our aim is to keep the Cultural Unit uniform. By uniform, I mean similar people with similar core values and ideologies." He was speaking slowly and intentionally, and I realized he was thinking before each sentence. After a short pause, he added, "I reckon you've already become familiar with the other student associations. We have several organizations in this college. They are all run by students but aren't totally independent of the university's authority. We believe the more independence from the governmental system, the more freedom and value our society has."

"Our society?" I asked hesitantly, slightly puzzled.

"Yes, our society, the Cultural Unit. The society could be our university, or, if you see the bigger picture, it is our city, our country." He smiled and turned to Karim. "Did you tell Nima about the uni during the last few years?" He glanced at Karim, looked at me and again turned to Karim without waiting for any answer.

Karim chuckled. "We didn't have much time to chat about everything. But I guess he's interested in literature and music."

I nodded, struggling to get my head around the discussion.

Ali smiled and continued, "Is that so? Good on you. I remember how difficult it was to get permission to run the literature and music divisions within the Cultural Unit." He puffed out a short sigh. "Oh man! Time flies so fast. It was three years ago." Ali smirked and added, "Boys and girls getting together and discussing music like what you saw today?! Not a chance, pal. It was an unforgivable sin! We were not allowed to carry out any musical performances, let alone hold any concerts."

I finally got what he was talking about. "I'm not from another planet, I'm aware of the severe religious restrictions," I said with a low tone, and shook my head.

Saber piped up. "Mashhad is the utmost religious city, and it is extremely difficult to express different opinions or do anything if they deviate even slightly from typical norms. I'm telling you, the barriers are unbelievably strict. We've been struggling for more than four months to get permission for one traditional Iranian music concert."

Ali jumped in. "Very well, enough for now. I'm starving. We have to go to the dorm's canteen for dinner. What's your plan, Nima? Karim just told me you don't live in the dorm?"

"No plan, but I'm gonna get back to my friend. I share an apartment with him. We are old pals from high school."

Ali smiled, took a magazine from the table, and led us out of the room. "That's great, man! See you later."

We shook hands, and they left in the opposite direction, toward the second exit at the back of the building.

The hallway was quiet, and I couldn't see anyone else there. I strode to the front door and headed out to the primary gate. It was a bright night with a few flashing stars scattered randomly in the sky. I took out my sweater from my backpack and put it on. For the first time, I was involved in an independent open discussion about society, politics, and culture. The exhilarating need to do something began to root all over my mind. I was not sure what, but I wanted to do something important, something that changed my routines and expanded my world. My brain was processing numerous ideas. At that moment, I couldn't tidy up my thoughts as they were all over the place.

"Where have you been? We're late!" Farid yelled at me when I unlocked the apartment door.

"What? I was at uni. Late for what?"

Farid wore a pair of jeans and a yellow jumper. His face was well-shaven, and his hair was shining under the ceiling lamp. He took his leather jacket and said, "Stay there! Don't come in. Let's go. Don't you remember? Your aunt invited us for dinner tonight."

"Oh, shoot! I totally forgot. Sorry. Let's go."

On the way to my aunt's place, I passionately told Farid about Ali, Saber, and Karim, recapping my meeting with them.

"They seem to be fairly reasonable and interesting fellas with decent knowledge about the political circumstances around the country. Their points of view were not like governmental hard-liners and right-wing conservatives. We haven't talked about politics too much, but I saw a black and white photo of Mosaddegh hung in the Unit. It is fascinating that the name of the organization is Cultural Unit, but whatever we touched on this evening, somehow ended up about politics!"

Farid was listening, nodding his head from time to time. "Um, interesting. What are they actually doing there? I mean, what are their priorities?"

I explained as many details as I knew until we arrived.

My youngest aunt and uncles were there, too, talking about their daily routines, the price of groceries, traffic jams, and the weather forecast for the weekend—as a typical family does. They asked us about the university and if everything was going well—same questions as last time, with the same answers! I signalled to my aunt that I wanted to call my parents, then dialled in and waited till my mother picked up the phone.

"Hi, Mom, it's me. Please call me back."

I hung up. If she called me, she would have to pay for the phone charges, rather than my aunt.

"You don't have to do that," my aunt scolded. "Please talk."

"That's fine, Auntie. It is better this way. Thanks."

Some moments later, my mother rang back. Talking with her always made me relax. I had yet to get used to living far from my hometown and family. It had only been a week. I repeated what I had told Farid about the Cultural Unit and ensured my mother that everything went very well over the first week.

After the phone call, we settled onto the couches with my family. My uncle asked Farid about our apartment and if we were fine with everything, while my aunt asked me if I had met any girls in our class.

My thoughts darted towards Taban, but I held my tongue. "Um…" was my lame reaction to her question.

She grinned while I was still thinking about Taban. My cousins were playing in front of the TV and my older uncle was repeatedly asking them to play in their room, so he could watch the evening news. We had dinner and stayed a bit more. Farid kept smiling and responding to random questions while glancing at me, begging to help him out. It was not too late, but we decided to leave and walk around Shahid Boulevard.

I could hear people's muffled voices upon leaving the apartment, and spotted the boulevard lights when we turned, crossing at the end of the alley. A group of boys, maybe the same age as us, were talking loudly together and sluggishly following three girls who were walking along the boulevard and looking into different shops, often giggling.

I poked Farid and showed him a restaurant with wide windows behind the girls on the other side of the boulevard.

"Look there. The place is packed with people. It should be a good one! Let's go and check it out."

"What? Are you still hungry?"

I laughed, "No, silly, just want to check it out for next time!"

Cars slowly crawled on both sides of the street, and from time to time, braked hard because of a red traffic light in the intersection or pedestrians crossing the street. Loud, fast pop music from a white Pajero SUV drew our attention. It was a bunch of guys who were chasing a couple girls in a red Honda sedan and trying to pass their phone numbers via the windows. Dodging left and right, we found our way through the maze of cars and crossed the street.

As we passed one storefront, Farid eyed at the flashy sign, then glanced inside the restaurant. "Pardis—cool name! We must try it next week."

I narrowed my eyes to get a better view of the inside of the restaurant while a noisy family with a stout boy who had a red balloon in his hand was standing in front of a folding glass door, trying to exit the restaurant.

Farid moved a bit and turned his face to the Boulevard again. It wasn't unusual to spot the same group of boys strolling along the Boulevard several times, eyeing girls within their age range, while the girls were glancing at the boys, whispering to each other and chuckling. It seemed everybody was aware of how to behave and react. It was like a harmonic interaction. Everyone had their own way to decode the mysterious desire for crossing the invisible red line, the undetectable barrier which was cultivated in each one's mind from childhood, and separated men and women everywhere.

"Oh, Mr. Zarin! What a pleasant surprise." Taban came out of the restaurant after the noisy family with a chubby boy.

Astounded, I paused for a couple of seconds. "Miss Pakzad! I did not recognize you."

Her outfit was different from what she used to wear in university. She was in a short-length outer garment that covered her body down to her knees with black jeans and a blue scarf that only sheltered half of her head. Her silky black hair was exquisitely pinned above her broad forehead. She was with another girl, who was a bit taller, with hazel eyes. She had similar clothes on, but with a green scarf.

"This is my friend, Asal. She's a beginner, too. Electrical Engineering Department."

Farid came along and introduced himself to Asal.

Taban was staring at me with her large shiny eyes as if she planned to hypnotise me. I wasn't sure what to say or what to do. I froze again but managed to mutter, "Um… we just had dinner at my aunt's home. Did you have dinner?" I regretted my words the second I asked the question. *She had just walked out of the restaurant—of course, she'd already eaten dinner, you idiot.*

Farid glanced at me, grinning, and then turned to Taban. "How was the restaurant? Is it worth a visit? Did you enjoy your time there?"

Taban just smiled. "Oh, yes, I liked it. It is a bit busy, but clean with decent service, good for hanging out."

"I liked the pizza. Yum! Taban ate a whole Margherita," Asal added with a soft voice.

We chuckled, staring at Taban like we knew each other for a long time.

"It was good to see you, guys," Taban said. "It's getting late, and we have to go. See you next week."

CHAPTER 3

I

Two months passed in the blink of an eye. Nights became longer, days became colder, and each morning, the horizon was covered with a thin blanket of fog. I was getting more familiar with the shortcuts around the university and the city both, just like the locals. The routines for students were simple: gathering in the café during breaks, going to the canteen for lunch, hanging around in college corridors, smoking in the front yard, or reviewing tutorials in libraries during long gaps between courses.

My routines were somehow different as I spent more time in the Cultural Unit, sitting around the table, chatting about random subjects with Ali, Jalal, Karim and Saber. Sometimes other folks joined the debates and shared their views, but the core team was almost always the same. Taban also visited the Unit frequently, showed interest in certain subjects and shared her opinions quite frankly. I felt different, in a weird desirable way, when Taban was there, sitting near me. Something was special about her, something inside her mind that distanced her from the other girls in the university.

It wasn't unusual to start a conversation about magic realism in fictional novels, the impacts of World War II on post-war literature, and ended up our session with how absolute

Islamic autocracy was giving power to right-wing hard-liners to suppress the reformist's party inside the government. I was like a sponge, soaking in every bit of information. The more I talked with other students, the more I realized how little I knew about everything.

December was around the corner when I somehow became involved in a political situation for the first time in my life. Although it was a tiny exposure, it soon escalated to an unprecedented chain of events that drastically changed my life. It all started when during one of our meetings in the Cultural Unit, Saber told me that the Ministry of Intelligence had arrested twelve activists at Tehran University, including some of his friends. They had been planning an anti-government vigil with the support of other students in the country, including us. The government forces had received a direct order from the Ministry of Intelligence to cease any political movements at all universities. Therefore, Saber gave me a heads-up to be cautious during the next couple of weeks, meaning no sharp political arguments, and no harsh critiques on religious views.

"The university's Islamic Council has been frequently calling over activist students these days. We must be more careful for a while," Saber said while we were walking with Ali to the canteen.

"What is the Islamic Council?" was my first question.

"The university's major governing authority for student associations. The student organizations are operating under their permission."

"What do you mean? Even the Cultural Unit or the Science Committee?"

"Correct. We all need the Islamic Council's permit for every single thing, like publishing magazines, holding book review sessions, offering training courses, and whatever else you can imagine!"

"Um, that sounds weird."

The next few days were a bit stressful for Ali and Saber. They were quieter than usual, and worried about their friends at Tehran University. Apparently, they had been interrogated by the government's Secret Service for two days before being released from custody. Not long afterward, all of them were expelled from the university. Ali and Saber were in close contact with other colleges in the city, regularly receiving updates from Tehran University on the next move; and the next move was tough but huge. The plan was to organize an integrated nationwide demonstration at all universities.

"First things first: raising awareness in our university," Saber told us after his meeting with the other Cultural Unit leaders.

"Why don't we plan a strike or demonstration now?" I asked.

"It is a marathon, not a sprint, pal. It may take years. We must be patient and cautious."

II

Dragging myself out of the bed, I eyed up at the tiny, opaque window, but couldn't figure out what the weather was like outside. I made a cup of instant coffee with boiled milk and knocked on Farid's door.

"Farid, get up. Time to go. We're gonna be late if you continue sleeping like a bear!"

A mumbling voice creeped out of his room, confirming that he was getting ready. Sipping my coffee, I walked back to my room to grab my textbooks for the day, mathematics, and physics.

"Where were you last night?" I asked Farid when he eventually left his room.

"Oh, man. I finally asked Asal out on a date."

"Are you kidding me?" I shouted, jumping out of my room.

"No kidding, buddy! I asked her out and she said yes!" Farid almost yelled. "We met after our last class while you rushed to visit Saber and Ali. We walked along the University Boulevard and headed to the Pardis restaurant early in the evening. Oh, buddy! It was amazing. Afterward, I walked her to the dorm and got back here a bit late. You were sleeping, I reckon." Farid explained the entire date with excitement. I never got to see him like that, waving his hands around and describing in such detail.

"That's awesome, pal! Was she with Taban?" I asked with a smile.

"Nope! You should ask Taban out. We can have a double date night!"

"Oh, man, I'd love to. I'm waiting for a perfect opportunity to ask Taban out on a date. Anyway, I'm very happy for you," I patted his back as we were about to head out.

"Asal is from Shiraz and came from a wealthy family. She wanted to immigrate overseas for higher education, but her dad didn't allow her. Her parents aren't religious, but I guess they are sort of traditional." He paused and headed out. "Oh, shoot it's raining!"

"Do you have an umbrella?"

"Nope!"

We walked out, knowing the rain would not stop soon. Speeding up to reach Abad Boulevard, Farid began to sing an old folklore song about falling in love under rainfall. I accompanied him by clapping and repeating the song under my breath. The only thought in my mind was to ask Taban out. *But how? And what would be her reaction?* A strange paranoiac thought in my mind pushed me away from asking her out on a date. I was afraid that she would refuse and start avoiding me afterward.

Rain droplets soaked my head with gentle coldness and found their way down to my neck. "That would've been lovely if Asal and Taban were here now! We could've started our band together!" said Farid, laughing and singing louder.

We were completely wet when we arrived at the university, so we ran to the toilet room straightaway. "Damn, no tissue to dry myself," Farid almost yelled.

I laughed. "Not much we can do, pal! Let's go to our class. We don't have much time."

"What a mess!"

Arriving in our classroom, I sat in my usual spot, the first seat of the first row in the right section of the room. It was like an aisle seat in the middle of the classroom. I didn't want anything to block my line of sight, especially a hairy neck. The class was half full with girls sitting on the left side and boys on the right, as usual.

"Didn't you two have an umbrella?" Taban asked me quietly while hardly trying to keep her face straight. She sat in the second row, behind me.

I turned back smiling. "I love rain! It washed away all dirt, making me fresh and clean. I can see the world clearer now."

Since we had met on the first day, I had taken every opportunity to catch up with her, whether short chitchat before our class, or a quick talk afterwards. But I did not have the courage to ask her out. In fact, I had never asked any girl out in my life. Something was different about her. She was confident when communicating with others, no matter boys or girls.

The mathematics professor came in and began to write formulas, numbers, and other symbols on the board, but my mind was somewhere else. I couldn't concentrate at all as it was like a hot pot of thoughts boiling inside my head. For an unknown reason, I was thinking about everything at the same time: *How's it better to ask Taban out? What's the new plan for the anti-government demonstration? Should I involve myself? Does Taban have the same feeling towards me? What should I do with my classes? I'm falling behind. I must ask her out.*

But what if she rejects me? What if she tells everyone? How can I join the literature group and attend music training? The sessions are at the same time. I'll have a hard time passing the mathematics exam…

Keeping my eyes on the professor's back, I sneaked out of the classroom. I just needed a short break to calm myself down. I stopped and looked around without searching for anything. The floor was made of clean white tiles, and there were six closed doors in the first hall, and then a long, bright hallway to another salon. Passing the other classrooms, I heard some random words, probably from the lecturers. From time to time, I glanced into the tiny door's window to see inside. It was the same picture each time—girls sitting on the left, boys sitting on the right, and professors writing on green chalkboards. I took the first staircase between the hall and the corridor, followed the steps three levels down to the foyer, and headed to the building's back door. Trying to organise my thoughts inside my head, I wandered towards the backdoor when I heard someone calling me.

"Nima! Nima, stop."

Only at that time I realized that the hallway was noisy and packed with students. Courses had been finished and everybody was in a short break till the next class. I turned back and there he was, Karim, approaching me.

"Karim! How's it going?"

"Hi! Where have you been? We've been looking for you all over the building. Farid said you marched out of the class before it ended." He paused and took out a small tissue from his pocket. Wiping his sweaty forehead, he continued, "Anyway, Babak wants to see you. Can you go to the Students' Science Committee? Do you have a class now, or are you free?"

"What?" I muttered. "Babak? Who is Babak? I've got to go to my physics class now."

Karim scratched his head as I picked up a hint of surprise in his face. "You don't know Babak? Um… He's leading the

Student's Science Committee. Head there straightaway after your class, please. He wants to talk to you about something important." Karim grinned, turned around, and walked away without waiting for my answer.

Great! He was smiling and clearly enjoying keeping me in the dark! I thought, then realized I needed to get going to my next class. *What's going on? Why didn't he say anything more? Why does Babak want to see me?*

Farid, sitting near my chair in the first row, rolled his eyes when I stepped into the classroom.

"Where the hell have you been, buddy?" He didn't wait for an answer before he continued. "You missed half of the class." He scanned my face, looking for a clue but soon gave up and said, "Karim was looking for you."

I dropped my backpack on the ground in front of my seat. "Oh, yes. I saw him downstairs."

"Are you going back to our apartment for lunch?" he asked.

I had not expected that question. "What?"

"What are you up to, buddy? We don't have any other classes today. Are you going back to our place after the tutorial, or do you have other plans?"

"Not sure! Karim asked me to meet some guy named Babak. No idea why," I answered as the professor entered.

"Okay, good, good. Don't come back till five o'clock, please," Farid whispered in my ear and winked.

I pretended looking at the chalkboard. "Oh, someone has a date at lunchtime! The sexy girl from Shiraz, the historical city of the most famous Iranian poets. Are you gonna read poems together, or you have other plans?"

"Shut up!" He grinned.

I smirked and poked him.

"Is there a problem there?" the professor questioned me, staring right into my eyes.

"Oh, sorry, professor. Nothing."

I glanced at Taban, fantasizing to invite her over.

She caught my glance and winked. Then she smiled, rose her index finger in front of her nose, hushing me with a teasing charm in her eyes.

III

Clumsily throwing a thick hardcover textbook, a folded notebook, and a couple of pens into my backpack, I rushed out of the classroom and darted to the Science Committee room. I zigzagged between boys and girls in the busy corridor, careful not to push them. The door was half-open when I got there, and I spotted Karim inside the room near the table. A girl with casual hijab and a guy were sitting around the table, chatting together. I had seen the girl in the Cultural Unit several times, but had never had a chance to introduce myself.

"Folks, this young man is Nima," Karim introduced, then turned to me. "Nima, this is Babak, and I believe you know Miss Anna Kordan? She's a member of our literature group in the Cultural Unit."

She was a tall, big-boned girl, with bright eyes, and who was in her second year of software engineering.

The loud background noise from the corridor suddenly disappeared as Karim swiftly closed the door. He smiled, waved his hand, and invited me to sit at the table. A bit baffled, I glanced at a pile of flyers on the other side of the table and a chaotic jumble of magazines near the computer desk on the other side of the room near the window.

"So, what's happening?" I asked Karim.

"Babak has been leading the Science Committee for several years. As you are aware, the election for new members will be in two weeks, and he's trying to finalize the candidate list for this year," Karim explained unhurriedly while the others stared at me. I guessed that they were all aware of the topic.

"Um, fair enough, but what does it have to do with me?" I replied cautiously as I didn't want to look like an idiot by asking stupid questions.

Karim glanced at Babak, smiled, and said, "Good question! Babak asked me the other day if I knew a trustworthy person to join them," he paused and mopped his forehead, "and you were the first name that popped into my mind." He then turned to Babak and added, "There you go. I think Nima can bring votes for the list! I'm gonna go now. I'll leave you alone to talk about whatever you want. I did my part!"

We shook hands and he left the room.

Babak was a slim boy with a sharp chin and olive skin. He wore a plain grey suit, which made him look a little older than the other students as not many students wore a suit at the university. He adjusted the thin, round, silver-framed glasses on his small nose and said, "I don't know Karim very well, but he's a kind pal, and always supportive. I was aware that he's dealing with many students, so I asked him if he knew someone from the beginners who was interested in joining our group."

I was somehow pleased by the situation as it felt satisfying to be recognized by Karim.

Anna listened while Babak briefly explained what was going on within the Science Committee. "What do you think? Are you in? Can we count on you?" he asked.

Anna stared at me and randomly flicked some flyers on the table.

I smiled and scratched my right eyebrow. "It sounds interesting. I'll think about it today and let you know by tomorrow morning."

Picturing myself as a member of the Science Committee who would be managing various scientific projects, I walked through the foyer and found myself in front of the Cultural Unit. The door was open, and my eyes caught a small crowd of students at the right corner of the room. I didn't wait or think more, marched in and waived at Karim who was chatting about book seminars.

The room was a bit darker than usual as someone had shaded the windows. Ali and Saber were at the other corner of the room, apparently talking about the anti-government protest at Tehran University. Although I listened carefully, it was not easy to follow the conversation.

A couple of minutes later, Karim finished his meeting with the other students and led them out of the room. He asked me about the Science Committee meeting. Ali and Saber stopped the conversation and stared at me unexpectedly.

"It sounds amusing! I probably accept the opportunity" was my answer.

"Great! You can assist us, then!" Saber added, rubbing his hands together.

I paused for a few moments. "Help you? What do you mean?"

Ali pushed the door and checked if it was closed. "Support us to cure the severely sick system. You can't imagine how restricted the university was some years ago. It wasn't like this a few years back! No one was even allowed to wear a pair of jeans here. It may be funny to you, but it wasn't like this when I started my education." He paused and gazed into my face like searching for something.

I shook my head, flabbergasted. "No, it isn't funny at all."

Saber picked up the conversation from where Ali left it. "During the last few years, we've been continuously demanding freedom of speech and constantly standing against the brutal censorship."

Ali patted me on my back. "Every single move must be approved by the Islamic Council. You name it—publishing a cultural journal, holding book review sessions, carrying out film critic workshops, facilitating a literature debate, organizing a music concert, and even planning a simple scientific tour for new students to visit the city power plant! Isn't it nonsense?! This situation must be stopped. And who can do that? Us! And only us!"

Karim jumped in this time. "Another similar case happened last year. We were under pressure to get a permit for a day trip to visit the Tomb of Khayyam and read some of his poems there. They didn't approve it because of the girls' attendance. Long story short, we didn't give up. We sent several requests and signed a petition. It finally worked, and they agreed on the tour."

Ali rubbed his left eye. "So, back to your question! How can you support us?" He paused for a second, making sure that I was following him. "Science Committee is part of this community and one of the student organizations in this society. If fanatic students took over the Committee, they would run the system backward. Do you see where I'm going with this? Everything is linked together. We need to protect ourselves and continue to build the place we are living in. This isn't only about our university. This links to all academic institutions around the country. We are in contact with them, too. The more resources in different units, the more support to achieve what we are aiming for, meaning removing the stupid restrictions. Sounds cliché, but trust me. This is the reality of our life now."

I listened to every word, putting them together in my mind and trying to analyse them simultaneously. I understood what they were talking about, but it was not easy to keep up with the pace and comprehend the deeper layers in that short amount of time.

IV

When I arrived at the Science Committee the next day, Babak was sitting at the table, drafting something with another guy.

"Have you met Borhan? He's been with the Committee for more than two years," said Babak, pulling up a chair for me to sit near them. Borhan was shorter than me and had curly black hair. His eyes seemed bigger behind the thick lenses of his burgundy wooden glasses.

"We're trying to finalize our list for the election. Have you made your decision?" asked Babak calmly.

I dropped my backpack near the table. "I'm in! How can I help?"

Babak smiled, "Awesome!" We shook hands.

Borhan gave me a piece of paper with some names on it. "This is the list of our candidates for this year. Five permanent members and three substitutes. Our friends told us that you are getting along with everybody, and you're easy-going." Borhan cleared his throat and continued, "In a nutshell, you're quite a charismatic face among beginners. So we picked you as the opening name."

I didn't understand the last part. "What do you mean by the opening name?"

"It means we want to write your name on top of the list. The first name," answered Borhan.

Babak picked up the confusion on my face and added, "This is a standard strategy for any election. We have a list, and the first name will catch the most eyes." He paused to see my reaction. "And show the bigger picture. For us, we want to let everybody know about having more new students on our team for this year. What do you think about the list?"

I, slightly puzzled, stared down at the paper. "1-Nima Zarin, Mechanical Engineering (98); 2-Babak Asgari, Civil Engineering (95); 3-..." My eyes froze on the third name. "3-Taban Pakzad, Mechanical Engineering (98)." I could not believe it. They nominated Taban, too. I didn't read the rest of the list. "Awesome!" was my sudden reaction.

"Congratulations! We have officially finalized our team," said Babak a bit louder than his usual tone and clapped his hands.

A few minutes later, after talking more about the election, we went to the canteen to have our lunch.

"I'm very optimistic for this year's election. We closed the perfect list, fifty-fifty," Borhan said quite confidently with a touch of patronizing gesture.

"What? Fifty-fifty? What do you mean?" I asked, looking at some guys in sport jumpers who were running around the football pitch.

"I mean, half of our list are ladies. This is the first time in this university that a nomination list has an equal number of female candidates on it. Miss Anna Kordan has a lot of experience from working in Cultural Unit. It was her idea." Borhan smiled, and his patronizing vibe dissipated like a faded plume from the tip of a cigarette.

Babak then described what we had to do before the election and when he was going to set up the first meeting between candidates, but I didn't listen to any of it as a torrent of new questions flooded my head from the moment I found Taban's name in the list. *How do they know Taban? When did they talk with her? Maybe Anna introduced Taban to the committee? Why didn't Taban tell me anything about her nomination when we talked about our activities at the university? Oh, boy! Taban and I, on the same list. This is amazing.*

Done with lunch, I headed to the dormitory to visit Abbas and Reza as we had a plan to review chemistry and mathematics for the upcoming exams. The men's dormitory had two types of flats—small ones with two single beds and standard rooms with two sets of bunk beds. Usually, small rooms were all booked by senior students. This is why Abbas and Reza were residing in a standard room with two other boys from our college. They were studying mathematics when I arrived. Abbas was on his bed, Reza laid on his side on the floor near the window, and the other two were sitting on the floor in front of the door on the faded carpet.

"Come on, guys! You are awfully boring! Enough with the studying. Let's go downtown and watch a movie, and afterward play billiards," I shouted, storming in.

Abbas laughed. "Oh, no. The earthquake is here!"

I patted Reza's shoulder and started to talk about the Science Committee and the upcoming election.

"Wow, that's awesome!" said Reza in a high pitch.

I clapped my hands and replied. "Oh, yeah, I'm so excited about it."

They all enthusiastically agreed to support me in promoting the list of nominated candidates. After studying mathematics for an hour or so, I wrapped up my stuff as I couldn't focus anymore.

"Guys! We must win. It is important to vote for the whole list," I said it for the third time since I got there.

"We got it, bro. Chill out! Sit down," Abbas answered.

"What time is it?"

"Um, about half past four. Why?"

"I'm gonna go now. But remember to ask everybody to vote for our list."

I yelled without knowing my voice was echoing in the corridor. Leaving the dormitory, I walked back to the college as I wanted to talk with Ali or Saber. A bit later, I was in front of the Cultural Unit, but I couldn't find anyone. Hanging around in the passageway, I glanced at the boards near the primary entrance and didn't notice anything new in the Cultural Unit section, but my eyes fixed on the Science Committee board as it was totally changed. A poster was now attached to the middle of the board and almost filled the entire area. It was the list with my name on top, and then came Taban's name.

I stared at my name and Taban's. On one hand, I was thrilled to experience a new responsibility, but on the other hand, I was concerned. *What would happen if we lost? If everybody got enough votes except me? Oh, no, that would be so embarrassing.*

The main hall wasn't busy at all. Two girls in black chadors passed the salon without looking toward the boards and a slender boy holding a few books in his hands ran up the stairs and disappeared in a few seconds.

Thinking about how to get more votes, I left the building. The cool, refreshing air combined with the frosty waft lifted my spirit. It wasn't dark yet, but the sun would set very soon. Still brainstorming, I was wandering down University Boulevard when I unexpectedly spotted Taban. My eyes went wide, and I took a closer look to make sure I was right. *Yes,* was the affirmative answer. There she was, standing at the end of the University Boulevard at the crossing to the park. I sped up, aiming to reach her before she took a cab.

"Hello, Miss Pakzad. Are you looking for a cab?" was my question which came out shaky as I needed to adjust my breathing.

She turned to me and paused for a moment, her eyes glittering. "Mr. Zarin. Yes, I am. Are you okay? You seemed to be out of breath?" She smiled and repeated. "Mr. Zarin?"

It was a ludicrous non-written cultural norm that men should not call women by their first name, and girls always used the boy's surnames unless they were family, or close friends. I really wanted to call her by her first name, *Taban,* to show her my pure emotions, but for no reason, I could not do that. I hated that stupid tradition.

"I'm fine, thanks. Where are you going, Miss Pakzad?" I asked her, trying to hide my excitement and adjust my fast breathing.

"Heading home. I'll take a cab to Abad Boulevard, then take a quick walk to my apartment."

"Me, too, the same way! I'd heard that you weren't living in the dorm. I'm not, either," I replied, this time firmly.

As I saw one pass, I waved my hand and stopped a public cab. Cabs were running in all directions, and anybody could get in. They were not like the private cabs that specifically drove passengers to one exact destination.

"So, you accepted a position on the list?" Taban asked while she was trying to roll up the window.

I nodded. "What a surprise for me to see your name on the list." I paused. "When did you nominate yourself? You didn't tell me." The last words released out of my control.

"Oh, Mr. Zarin. It all happened so fast. It is fascinating to experience new things. You are so active. You attend all the events. I liked it," she answered in a friendly tone, trying to change the subject.

"Not all. Mostly literature and music. Sometimes film and poetry, too."

"How do you find enough time for all these things and study your courses, too? Exams are close and I'm a bit nervous about them."

"Um…" I sighed. "There's not enough time at all. I cut out several sessions and I'm way behind the classes, but I just can't give up on other activities. I like literature more than mathematics, and music more than physics. This place is packed with lots of opportunities."

"You are right. But we have to pass these exams, too! Actually, that should be the priority!" She chuckled, so did I.

"I know. I know. You are right. The first exam is mathematics, and I've missed a couple tutorials. What about you? Are you on top of all the courses?" I asked, trying to continue our conversation as much as possible.

I didn't want it to end. *Should I ask her out now? How? Oh boy!* The cab stopped to pick up another passenger. A girl in a black chador opened the back door. Taban moved to the left and sat in the middle seat, right next to me, so the girl in chador could get in the cab and sit near the window. Trying to slow down my fast heartbeats by berating deeply I sensed that I was about to blush. The cab moved before the girl in chador shut the door. Taban shifted a bit to my side and her left arm touched mine. My palms sweated as something like flame unexpectedly flashed inside me. I floated in her soft perfume and sensed her warm body. I tried to ask her the same question again and controlled myself to not blush or tremble or sweat.

"Um… so, I'm sure you are so ready for the exams?"

She smiled and gazed at me. "Not really, but the girls have been studying together at the library. I also bought a supplementary mathematics book. It is quite helpful. One of the senior students recommended it to me." She searched her bag, took out a thin green book, and gave it to me. "There you go. You can have it this weekend. Extra examples with key methodologies. I don't need it till next week. Take a look. I hope it helps."

"Thanks. Very kind of you, Miss Pakzad. I'll certainly read and bring it back in one piece early next week."

Taban chuckled and a moment later asked the driver to stop.

"Let me pay," she suggested, and did not wait for my answer before paying for both of us.

This was an extremely uncommon gesture— pleasingly odd. I was puzzled and my tongue acted before my brain. "Um, well, no problem!" I muttered watching her hand passing the money to the cab driver.

The chauffeur glanced at me in the mirror as she left the cab, but I ignored the look. Instead, I eyed the green mathematics book again, touching the cover with the tip of my fingers. *She likes me, too. I'm sure.* I wondered about the person who recommended the book to Taban. *She said a senior student. Was it a guy or girl? It could not be a man! Please!*

I looked outside through the window and realized that I had been so entrenched in my thoughts that I had forgotten to ask the driver to stop at my place. "Oh! I'm getting out here. Please pull over." I walked back, disappointed at myself for not asking Taban out when I had had a perfect shot. *You are an idiot!*

Farid was lying in front of the TV reading a weekly sports magazine when I arrived. It seemed that his guest, Asal, had left an hour ago.

"How was your date, pal?"

"It went pretty well. She brought a box of Merci chocolate. Help yourself."

I laughed, glanced at the open chocolate box on the kitchen table, and searched for a pistachio one. Unwrapping the chocolate bar, I began to explain the ballot system, candidate list, advertisement, rally, and the importance of winning the election. I kept chatting with Farid as I stepped into my room, opened my backpack, and pulled the green math book out. Farid left the sports magazine on the sofa and followed me while he was listening to my daily report.

He was a good friend. Although he had had quite a rough childhood because of his parents' divorce, he had never shown any sign of weakness or complained of anything. I truly admired his personality, and he was a kind of a role model for me to stop grumbling around. In spite of the fact that he was a people person, he wasn't interested in getting involved in many events at the university.

"So, are you going to be the busiest man at the university?" he asked after a short pause. "Who are the other candidates? Any chicks there?"

I puffed out a laughter. "Half the list are girls. One of them is Miss Pakzad."

Farid rose his right eyebrow and grinned. "So…" He paused as his eyebrow rose more and his grin became clearer. "So, this is the reason you're doing it! You had a crush on her from day one." He dropped himself on my bed.

"It may sound corny, but she is kind, charming and different from the others," I answered with a trembling voice, avoiding looking back at him.

Farid could not stop beaming. "Good luck! You have all my support, buddy! In both ways— the election *and* Miss Pakzad!" He poked me several times and left the room while softly singing the "Lady in Red" song.

I pushed the door with my foot, laid on my bed, and flipped through the green math book page by page. Instead of reading the calculation guidelines and memorizing the essential formula, I eyed at the footnotes and other scripts that Taban had written in it. Her handwriting was meticulous, all the letters were flawlessly the same size, all words in italic format on an invisible straight line. Scanning the notes, I found a part of a famous Iranian poem inside the cover.

"Every day and night I'm asking myself,
Why am I negligent about my true feelings?
Where do I come from? Why was I brought here?
Where am I eventually heading to?
Why don't you show me my homeland?"

That had been one of my favourite poems during teenagehood. I repeated it over and over. The poet, Rumi, was pleading to comprehend the ultimate reason of life, questioning the goal of the existence of human beings.

Suddenly, it hit me that although I had read this poem many times in the past, I had never had the courage to go deeper and question the religious beliefs that society had carved in my mind during my childhood. I had been born and raised in a country with an absolute Islamic autocracy that was entirely governed under altered harsh Islamic rules. I could have been brainwashed, filled with nothing but religious rules and dark superstitions. I was so fortunate to have open-minded parents who taught me how to think about everything and question the unknowns, even if asking about the subject was forbidden.

Reading that poem, thinking about the last eighteen years of my life, and everything I had seen in the last three months at the university was like a spark in a gunpowder depot. I could not stop reminiscing about the past, thinking about the present, and dreaming about the future as my mind wildly flew through time, into history. Going back a thousand years ago, I thought about myself, my world, my life as if the chain of events had been different. *The great Persian empire, the invasion of Persia by Muslims, the disintegration of the realm, Iran before the Islamic Revolution, my homeland after the Islamic Revolution, the eight-year war between Iran and Iraq, my kindergarten, primary school, intermediate school, high school, and now university. What could have happened if one of these events had ended differently? How would I live now if the Islamic Revolution had not succeeded? Why am I in this world? What is the ultimate reason for my life? What is going to happen after death?* Scattered questions and random thoughts stormed in my head, and I was completely unable to stop them. That was one of those first moments—the first time I genuinely questioned the philosophy of life. It was the first time I doubted everything I had ever heard, learned, or been exposed to until that very moment. Something was about to change, and I felt it all, but I was not able to understand a bit of it; I was paralysed to comprehend it. It was at that moment when I decided to seriously search for the real purpose of life, deeply and vigorously questioning the unquestionable. *Yes, yes I must read more and more and more. The first step is to ask the forbidden question: Does God exist?*

CHAPTER 4

I

For the next two weeks, I was swamped with promoting our candidate list and getting ready for the election day, attending literature workshops, following the latest news from the protest at Tehran University, practicing music, researching religions, and studying for the final exams. I was worried about things spinning out of my control.

It was the night before the Science Committee election. I wasn't in the mood to stay alone in our apartment as Farid had a plan to hang out with Asal, probably at a café or restaurant—I didn't ask, and he didn't tell me more. *I wish Taban was here now. Where is she? What is she doing?* Imagining Taban and I together in the Science Committee, I took a deep breath and puffed it out with force, grabbed my backpack and decided to catch up with Babak.

It was not a freezing evening, so I preferred to walk and window shop on Shahid Boulevard before heading to the dormitory. Colourful shops, twinkling lights, and crowded places always made me relax and helped to relieve stress. Strolling around, I saw a girl in front of a fancy boutique, facing the flashy interior decoration. She was quite slim with a blue scarf on her head. *Oh! She must be Taban?* I thought cheerfully and smiled. Planning inside my head how to surprise her, I carefully walked towards her. She stared at something behind the shoe shop's window and turned back to me before I stepped closer to her. It was like I hit a concrete wall as the girl gave me an annoying look and headed into the shoe shop, left me with an embarrassing shade of disappointment. *Oh, boy. I wish she were Taban. What's Taban doing now?*

Babak was in his room when I got there. He was playing cards with some other guys whom I had met a couple of times in the Science Committee room. A thin cloud of grey smoke was drifting out of a tiny opening in the window where a small metallic plate full of cigarette butts laid on the dusty shelf.

I asked Babak if everything was going well, and if we were ready for the following day.

His answer was brief: "Yes, I hope so."

The guys kept playing cards without bothering to make eye contact with me. It was like I was not welcome to stay for more than a few minutes, so I shortened my uninvited visit and left his room. The hallway was sharply illuminated by fluorescent lamps. I couldn't understand if it was only my inner perception, or if the eye-scratching whiteness of the dormitory's fluorescent lamps was intrinsically depressing. Ambling there, I took the stairs up to the third floor with the hope to boost my mood by visiting Ali and Saber. I knocked a few times and waited behind the closed door, listening to figure out if anyone was inside the room. A few seconds later, I heard some weak clacking noises, then the jingling sound of key inside the lock, and not long after, Saber opened the door.

"Surprise!" the word came out of my mouth dimly.

"Hi, buddy. What are you doing here? Come on in." Saber smiled, leading me in.

Holding an empty mug in his hand, Saber seemed quite funny in his red hatched pyjamas. Water was bubbling noisily inside an electric kettle and rumbling steam was flying away from the spout.

"Oh! What are they doing?" was my question to Saber when I noticed Ali, hunching behind the table and drafting something like an announcement. Jalal was sitting near him, double-checking the texts.

"Am I interrupting something?" I asked.

Saber briefly explained their plan to organize a demonstration against the recent menacing environment in the university, which had started after Tehran University's sacking of twelve of its students.

Saber asked, "Want a cup of tea?"

"No, thanks. I'm gonna go soon. I just visited Babak to make sure everything is alright for tomorrow."

Ali calmly said, "Oh, man. Chill out! Many students already confirmed they would vote for you. Don't worry, pal."

Saber seconded him with confidence and poured tea for everybody. He cracked some jokes and then talked about a girl he had a crush on a long time ago. He hadn't been able to get to her because of the obvious gap between their lifestyles. Sipping his tea, he asked if I was seeing someone, not as though he was curious, but to keep the conversation going.

"Um, not really."

Ali and Jalal wrapped up whatever they were doing and joined us.

"Not really? What does that mean?" asked Jalal, grinning.

II

It was late evening when I unlocked the door and sneaked into the apartment. No lamp was on, so I assumed Farid was sleeping. I waited for a few seconds till my eyes adjusted to the darkness inside our underground flat, then soundlessly found the way to my room and swiftly turned on the light. A few lines of brightness escaped outside of my room, making the living room a bit visible. It was then I realized that Farid wasn't in his room as his bedroom door was open.

"Farid?" I said quietly. No answer came back. "Farid?" this time I called him loud and clear. *Where is he? Why is he not back yet?* I was a bit worried, but there was nothing I could do at that time. I headed to my bed and tried to sleep, hoping he would be back soon.

The night went by with a hodgepodge of dreams—or maybe nightmares—that I couldn't remember the next morning. I woke up early, still tired, and the first thing I did was check out Farid's room. The empty bed was not what I'd been hoping for. *Where the hell is he? He probably slept over in Abbas's room.*

I got ready in a rush and stormed out to the not-so-busy street, before suddenly pausing and taking a moment to indulge myself with the warmth of the early sunshine, letting the refreshing, chilly morning breeze caress my whole body. Passing a couple of alleys, I arrived on Abad Boulevard. Quivering amber leaves on almost-dried branches had no choice but to accept their destiny and circled down to the ground from towering, half-naked plain trees on both sides of the street. The last sound of autumn was the voice I loved to embrace my ears when I deliberately took my steps on the carpet of dry leaves.

We must win the election. Both of us, me and Taban together, was the dominant thought in my head while trying to hasten and reach the university sooner. It was about eight o'clock when I arrived at the Engineering College. Not many people were around as I had expected, but I spotted Abbas and Reza passing in front of the doorway.

"Hey you two, freeze!" I ran toward them, shouting not too flashy.

"Good morning to you, too!" answered Abbas, followed by a short laughter. "Don't worry, we'll vote for you!"

"I love you, guys!" I said with a grin. "Where is Farid?" I asked, hoping that my presumption was correct.

"What?" asked Reza a bit confused. "Farid? He's your roomie, not ours!"

"He didn't bloody come back home last night."

"What do you mean?" Abbas asked.

I murmured, "Shit… Where is he, then?"

"Don't worry, buddy," said Reza, followed by a long yawn. "We're going to have our breakfast in the café. Join us. Maybe Farid will show up soon."

There was only one car in the parking area. I glanced back at University Boulevard; not many people there, either. "Fine," I rubbed the back of my neck and accompanied them to the café.

"We booked two PCs from nine to eleven o'clock," Abbas told me before ordering his breakfast.

A familiar traditional song, playing from a small radio behind the cashier, kept my mind busy for a few seconds with the guessing game, but I couldn't remember its name.

"What are you going to work on?" I asked Abbas while we waited for our orders.

"Microsoft Word," he answered and took out a thick book from his brown messenger bag. "This is what we're gonna read today." He then handed the book over to me.

"This is awesome!" I replied with childish excitement. "I want to learn it, too. Everybody is talking about it these days. Rumour has it that the entire university administration may change their system and use this software for typing their letters."

Reza smiled. "So, join us. Let's go together."

I wasn't surprised by the invitation, as they were always supportive and kind to me. "Oh, not today. It is the election day. I must be on the floor to keep my eyes on the polling station. I hope to find Farid soon, too! Guys, I'm worried about him."

Breakfast was ready. I had ordered two fried eggs garnished with sliced and pickled cucumber, fresh tomato wedges and a super-thin white bread called *lavash*. It was undoubtedly the most famous dish in the entire university. Breaking the yolk with the tip of my fork, I asked Abbas, "When are you going to make me an email address? You promised me to do it last week."

Abbas sipped up his tea. "Find ten minutes this morning and join us in the computer room. We'll make it together. It's easy and doesn't take too much time."

I smiled and patted his back. "My man! See you there."

I had finished my breakfast in haste like someone was pushing me and headed to the Science Committee room. Babak was already there, in his grey suit. His friends were also in the room, chatting about yesterday's football match between their favourite teams.

"Need a hand?" I asked amicably.

"Thanks, buddy. The ballot box has been set up in the main salon, and we'll start in five minutes, at nine o'clock sharp," Babak answered, then he winked at his friends, and we left the room together.

As we passed the corridor, I eyed at two men who didn't seem to be students, standing near the locked polling box in the hall. My guess was that they were supervisors from the university election centre, but I didn't ask Babak as we almost reached them in a few seconds. One of them wore a plain white shirt with all the buttons fastened up to his neck, and the lower part untucked and loosely left out of his brown cotton trousers, typical governmental attire. He had a short black beard. Babak shook hands with them, and they unlocked the ballot box. Babak glanced inside, and then they sealed it. The election was officially started.

I stood in the salon, watching who was coming and going, looking for familiar faces to ask for the vote. *Maybe Farid will walk in soon? Where is Taban? We must win.* It was almost quiet at that time, but the closer to lunchtime, the more students gathered at the main hall and cast their votes.

Strolling around the ballot box, in the corridors and the upper floors, I enthusiastically asked everyone if they had voted or not. "Have you cast your vote yet? It is the Science Committee's election day. Please vote for our list!" I repeated these sentences over and over until a loud voice hit my ears from behind as someone frequently calling my name. I turned swiftly. It was Saber storming towards me.

"What's up, buddy?" I did not wait for the answer and asked the next question. "Have you voted yet?"

Saber dragged me out of the building near the backyard where no one could hear us.

"Nima, what are you doing? You have to stop it," he said with a solemn look on his face.

"What? I don't understand. Stop what?"

"You're not allowed to promote your list on election day. They are about to report your team. The Basij Organization is going to file a complaint because you are promoting the candidates on election day." Saber explained the circumstances without losing his temper.

I was quite shocked, as I had not understood the severity of my behaviour. "I didn't know that. No one told me. What do you mean by a complaint? What's going to happen now?"

"We took care of it, and the case didn't get through the election board."

"That's good. Yes? How?"

"Don't worry about it, pal. Just stop it. I gotta go now. Good luck!"

"You saved my day!" I puffed out a trembling breath and roughly scratched my head.

Patting my back, Saber winked at me and left.

For no particular reason, I was afraid of going back to the ballot zone, so I kept lingering near the café until I remembered Abbas and Reza. *They're supposed to be in the computer room.*

I sneaked into the building and took the stairs to the fourth floor where the computer room was located. It was a spacious salon with about forty computers around the room and a few printers against the wall near the door. I handed over my student ID card to the computer room supervisor and entered. All spots had been taken as students from different departments were working on the stations. The dot-matrix printers made an intermittent noise like a needle scratching a rough surface while the dial tone of connecting to the Internet was kind of strange. Looking around, I found Abbas and Reza sitting near each other in the corner of the room. "Okay, okay, enough with the fancy information technology things, let's make me an electronic mailbox!"

They laughed and asked me about the election. "How's it going down at the voting pole?"

"I've got a warning! They told me to leave the premises!"

They chuckled and thought I was kidding.

"Bullshit! Just a moment, and I'll make you an email address. Have you found Farid?" Abbas asked.

"No," I replied.

He closed some folders and files on the monitor, then asked the supervisor for Internet connection. "Station nine, please."

After a minute, the dialling sound came out from the back of the computer. A series of blinking small blue boxes between the image of a phone and a satellite dish appeared in the centre of the screen.

"What name do you want for your email?" Abbas asked as he double-clicked the Internet Explorer icon, trying to bring up the Yahoo website.

"Not a clue! What about 'Nima's First Email'?"

"The official mailbox address is often your full surname."

"Sounds fine to me. Go for it!"

I pulled over a chair to sit closer to the monitor. It took about twenty minutes while Abbas walked me through the basics and showed me how to write a new message, attach a file, and send the email. I had had a computer while I was in high school, but everything about the Internet was new to me. When it was ready, I pointed at the sealed letter envelope's image in the inbox section. I got so excited about having my first electronic communication. The intriguing concept of connecting to the whole world charged me like I found a way to fly to wherever I wanted.

"This is an auto-message from Yahoo admin," Abbas explained. He briefly taught me how to work with the system, and then asked me to send him a file as a practice. I clicked the new message item, but nothing happened.

"No Internet connection."

"Oh shoot, the Internet credit ran out. I booked one hour and spent it all."

"Fine. No problem. I'll practice another time. Thanks a lot, mate. Catch you later."

I left the computer room and walked to the Cultural Unit. Saber and Jalal were sitting around the table, quietly reading something. I took a seat on the opposite side of the table and stretched my hands over my head. They paused and looked at me without a comment. I moved a bit on the chair and asked, "Have you seen Farid around?"

Saber smiled. "He's fine. He slept the night behind the bar. But don't worry. He's with Ali now."

"What?!" The question came out of my mouth louder than I'd expected, and my eyes widened in puzzlement.

"Police caught him with his girlfriend yesterday when they were walking along University Boulevard."

It was usual for police or Islamic militia to wander around and catch young boys and girls who were hanging out, if the girl and boy were not married together. It was part of the government's rules.

"Shit. Is he alright? I've told him many times to be careful." I chewed my lower lip. "By the way, how do you find out all this, and why he is with Ali now?"

"You don't have a phone. Farid called the dormitory this morning. Ali went to the police station and bailed him out. They should be coming over soon."

A bitter blend of pity and rage twirled inside me, not against Farid but the governing system. "I've told him a hundred times to not walk with Asal in such places. The police are always manoeuvring there, trying to catch boys and girls. Where is Asal now?"

"Apparently, she's signed a sort of commitment paper and got out last night. She must be back at the dormitory. She was so upset as the police called her parents last night."

"Oh, that's not good."

"No, it is not. Miss Pakzad is with her now."

"Miss Pakzad? So, this is why she didn't show up yet for the Science Committee election. How do you know that?"

"Babak told Jalal, and Jalal told me."

"Babak?" I paused. "At least they are fine, I mean Farid and Asal. That's a relief. I was worried." I cleared my throat and asked, "How's the election going?"

"Apparently your list is ahead for now."

I clapped my hands. "I can't wait to see the final results."

The election due time was four o'clock, but it had been extended till six by the election board. Outside, it was getting dark and a bit frosty. I stood in the salon, far from the ballot box but near the Cultural Unit board, trying to calm myself by reading an article about the fundamentals of feminism. Anna had written it, and Saber had attached it to the board. I couldn't focus on the article as guessing about the election results shadowed my thoughts like a giant thundering cloud; so, I gave up reading it after a few paragraphs. Instead, I eyed Babak and some other guys who were talking adjacent to the polling station. Everybody was waiting to wrap up the election and stride to the amphitheatre to counting the votes. A few minutes later, Taban and Anna approached Babak. I couldn't hear them as few students were hanging around in the salon, but it was obvious that they were talking about the day and election, or at least that was my guess. I could see Taban talking with passion, waving her hands, and laughing all together. A hypnotising sentiment of jealousy prevented me from joining them. Something bizarre from inside held me back. It was not more than five minutes, but I felt it like hours, until Taban and Anna left the salon and then I joined Babak. A few minutes later, we left the building to head to the amphitheatre together. Although I was burning to ask what Taban had been laughing about, I controlled myself and said some nonsense about weather temperature change from early morning till night.

The ballot box arrived just a few minutes after we entered the designated area in the amphitheatre, and the counting started without any delay. Every vote was read two times by different men from the election board and the numbers were recorded on a whiteboard behind them. I was delighted each time I heard my name, "Mr. Nima Zarin," but tried to behave myself, and not show any sign of joy. Halfway through the counting, I slightly calmed down as Babak was first in the tally, and I was second. But Taban's vote count was still marginal. It was difficult for women to get the required ballot count; however, she had more votes than most of our rivals.

"What do you think? Can we all get through? Miss Pakzad seems to need more votes," I whispered under Babak's ear.

"Don't worry. She'll have enough votes. I know."

"Really? How do you know?"

"Because I know!"

He stared back at the whiteboard and smiled.

Borhan was alone on the other side of the salon. He caught my glimpse and waved his hand. *He seemed quite confident, too,* I thought, waving back.

The counting was approaching its end, and we were sure that six out of eight from our list, including Taban, Anna, and

Borhan would be taking seats in the Science Committee for the academic year.

The soothing waft of success carried me away for a few minutes. Thinking about future responsibilities, spending more time with Taban, sharing works together, and picturing new experiences kept me charged until I reached my apartment. Only then did I realize how exhausted I was.

Farid was already sleeping in his bed, and I did not wake him up. I slowly shut his door, smiled, and tiptoed to my bed.

III

The upcoming days were enjoyably hectic. I liked the torrent of new tasks and actions around me. We had at least one or two meetings in the Science Committee every day. I gladly attended all of them as I could spend more time with Taban and share some common activities together while I got familiar with what was going on at the Science Committee. On top of that, I had to get myself ready for final exams. We were rapidly approaching the end of first semester, and I was quite behind on my tutorials. Despite having all these things on my plate, I did not miss a single session of the Cultural Unit's literature workshops while still working on my research about religions. Ali asked his friends to support me with some courses while Farid frequently reminded me to focus on the upcoming tests.

"Would be helpful if I could stretch the day!" I said to Farid during one of our chitchats on our way to the university.

The handover between the Science Committee ex-members and the new team took place a week after the election. Babak explained how we should select the roles for each fellow, namely the committee leader, executive manager, financial manager, and administrative lead. He discussed the responsibilities and proposed nomination for every position. "Executive manager has the most responsibility here, even more than the leader.

Everything is in his or her hands, from handling the publication of our magazine to organizing factory visits. We need someone active, smart, and reliable. Someone who has the ability to get the job done, and I believe Nima is fit to take this duty perfectly." Babak winked at me swiftly. I was flattered and obviously liked the idea. He explained that the roles of leader and financial manager could be combined under a single title. We didn't have any doubt about him remaining the committee leader.

We took a quick poll on the same day, and everybody agreed on the assigned responsibilities. The title of manager was fancy and exciting. Babak wrote my name and my new title—committee executive manager—and asked me to sign the meeting draft. Taban became the admin lead. The role needed considerable relationships with different parties.

"I'll help you to get familiar with our connections inside and outside the uni, Miss Pakzad," Babak ensured Taban.

"Thanks, Mr. Asgari. I'm looking forward to it," Taban answered with a gentle smile, and her large, gleaming eyes paused on Babak for some moments.

A sudden jealousy hit me again, not long, just for a second, like something was pressing against my throat.

"I'll type it out and send the official minutes of the meeting to the university election board tomorrow morning," said Babak in his typical calm voice and wrapped up the meeting by handing each of us a key. "The last person out, remember to turn off the lights and lock the room, please. I gotta go now. See you tomorrow morning."

I was still sitting near the table, looking at the new key in my hand, while the others packed up their stuff and left the room.

"Are you ready for the mathematics exam?" Taban asked me while she put her small notebook in her burgundy purse.

"Oh, absolutely not!" I chuckled, "Farid told me the boys would study together this afternoon. I need to be at the dorm in an hour. What a mess! Tomorrow math, Monday chemistry. And the worst is yet to come—physics! What about you?"

"Huh… come on, Mr. Zarin." Her white teeth sparkled as she burst a cute laughter. "It's not that difficult, but you need to practice with complex integrals and finite limit. I've heard half of the questions are from those chapters."

"How do you know that, Miss Pakzad? It seems you got it from a trustworthy source. Are you spying on teachers?" I grinned, as I kept staring at her eyes.

"I just asked a senior student who had already passed these courses. He described how each professor selected the questions."

"Oh!" I tried to hide my jealousy. "You have connections everywhere. Now I understand why you became the admin lead!"

We shared a short laugh. Leaving the room, I turned off the lights and she locked the door. I always stayed a bit longer in the Science Committee room after the meetings and asked Taban some questions about whatever popped in my mind as I wanted to spend more alone time with her.

"Thanks for the hint. I'm gonna go to the dorms now. See you tomorrow," I said while my mind was somewhere else. *A senior student? He? Who is this guy? Are they just friends?*

The corridor was quiet when I eyed around and saw just a couple of students who had come out of the Basij Organization room and walked to the salon. The Cultural Unit door was closed and most of the courses had been finished by that time. A small group of students stood near the back door, talking with their young professor. I walked toward them and headed to the dormitory while my brain struggled to forget about the senior-guy student who had helped Taban. I had a shaking intuition that Taban and I were getting closer, or at least that was what I hoped. *Who is this unknown man? Why am I so jealous? She is always asking me about my courses.*

She cares about me! It was a new sensation for me, something like a fluffy, velvety blanket that kept me warm. But that was not all I felt. Something like jealousy was needling me from inside, too.

IV

First semester finished, and the final exams did not go as well as I had anticipated or hoped. I didn't tell my parents about it, but instead I talked about my new responsibilities in the Science Committee and how busy I was. Most students took a short winter break to visit their hometowns. Farid bought a return train ticket and insisted I join him. "I'd love to come with you, pal, but Science Committee's activities are too much, and I have to sort them out before the new semester. Even Babak is staying here. I promised to help him."

I was not lying, but that was far from the only reason. I deliberately kept myself busy by spending most of my time facilitating a day trip to a sugar factory for the next semester, preparing the new issue of the committee's magazine, and planning for the upcoming term's software training courses. The real reason, though, that I wanted to stay at university during the winter break was something else—or rather, *someone* else.

A few days before exams, Babak had told me that Taban would be staying in the city during the winter break to help him with the Science Committee. I was a bit upset at first and tried not to show my emotions. *I should stay! Taban will be here, and we can catch up more.* The Science Committee's workload for the new semester was the perfect excuse to get along with her often and share some moments together. The university was not crowded, and we could meet each other without repeatedly being interrupted by others. *This is the time! I should ask her out. I must!*

Taban and I frequently met up at the university to chat about our daily routines and often walked back to our places together during those days—moments of happiness, I called them. It made me warm during those cold short days and left me alone with a bunch of innocent childish dreams at long night. I did not understand why, but due to some unknown reason, I still didn't dare to ask her out. Something always blocked my mouth when I thought about revealing my true feelings for her. An invisible suffocating force pressed against my chest and gripped my throat every time I was about to invite her for a dinner, or to suggest we go to cinema together, or anything else. A hideous, immature shame had always given me cold feet whenever I stared into her eyes and planned my imaginary date.

V

The short winter break came to its end fast, and the new semester started. I had planned the sugar factory visit for January. Although the budget was approved by the university commercial department, we had not received the permit from the Islamic Council. Babak had been trying to get the permit over the winter break, but apparently, they had not responded to his request. He told me that he couldn't get the money from the college finance team until the council approved the tour.

"What's the problem? Why is it taking so long? The permit should have been ready last week," I asked Babak furiously in our first weekly meeting of the new semester.

He moved his hand away from his face and took a long breath. His eyes were narrowed behind his glasses.

"The problem is we've planned for a day trip, girls and boys together. The Islamic Council called it a 'mixed journey.' This isn't something they like. They are against the mixed tours, and we have no power to proceed without their approval."

"So, what should we do? Just wait? I've busted my arse off during the winter break to manage this educational trip. Additionally, the factory's coordination centre made it clear that the only free time for students to visit would be Thursday next week."

Babak scratched his forehead.

"Calm down, buddy." He paused for a second. "Um… I reckon the only way is to let either boys *or* girls go. One team only. Then we can organize another trip later. This is what we always do. It costs more money, but who cares, they'll pay!"

I didn't say anything for a few moments, thinking about Babak's suggestion. Eyeing around the room, I shared a glance with Taban, and then turned back to Babak.

"What if we go apart? Rent two buses. Boys with boys and girls with girls. In that case, we can change the request to two separate trips."

Babak rose his head and gazed at me.

"Um… not a bad idea." He glanced at Borhan and turned to me again. "But it's a bit tricky, buddy. It just may work. We must send two individual requests. Um… First, the permit for boys, which is easier to get approval for, and the day after, a new request for girls."

"Sounds like a plan to me!" I said it sharply.

A week later, we got into two separate buses and headed to the sugar factory not far from the city. The boys' bus left from the dormitory and girls' from the university's central gate. Farid and I sat near each other in the first row, talking about our new friend, Amin. We had met him a few days back at Pardis restaurant when he was having his dinner with Ali and Saber. Amin was a tall, muscular, well-dressed guy with bushy light brown hair who had been born in Mashhad and had commenced his academic education in our college a year before us.

"I liked him. He's cool," Farid said quietly.

"Yes, he seems like a nice pal. Ali told me that Amin is helping them a lot," I said while glancing at the back of the bus. Babak was sitting with a couple of students from other classes, chatting and bursting out with laughter.

"Did you know he has a mobile phone?" asked Farid.

"Who? Amin? Yes, I saw it in the restaurant the other night. He must be from a wealthy family."

The mobile phone system had only started to operate in Iran just some years before I entered the university, and only a tiny portion of society could afford it at that time.

It took about two hours to reach the factory and ten minutes later, the girls' bus pulled up beside ours.

"Hi, Miss Pakzad. How was your ride? All good?" I asked Taban when she got out of the bus with her hand on her head, tightening her casual hijab, a dark blue scarf over her hair.

"Good day, Mr. Zarin! Well, everything is going as planned thanks to the executive manager." She winked at me, then walked to Babak and passed him the list of girls on the bus.

Asal got out of the bus and swiftly waved her hand at Farid, but did not get closer to him. They had sort of split up after the police had arrested them. It wasn't something they wanted, but her father was against their relationship and had pushed her to stop seeing Farid.

A few minutes later, a man in his mid-forties approached us and introduced himself as the factory shift supervisor's assistant. He led us to the front yard and started explaining sugar processing from the beginning. We all pointed at different equipment and whispered around walking in a muddled queue. Everybody was thrilled about the first academic excursion. The tour continued in the parking lot, where trucks were delivering sugar canes and beetroots. Then we passed the storage area and washing system. A bit later, the shift supervisor's assistant directed us from the warehouse to the production unit. Enormous vessels of molasses, conveyors, mixers, and packing devices were all set up in a massive production area with enormous white lights on the ceiling. A weird, pungent smell that I had never experienced before was all around the place as I walked with Abbas and Farid at the end of the line, and often leaning to right or left looking for Taban among the other girls. Abbas had a decent knowledge of sugar refining and occasionally gave us extra information. "This is an unrefined batch. The smell and colour are so different," Abbas explained while the entire group stopped near the packing machines where the supervisor's assistant described the delicacy of time management and weight control while we broke the queue like kids in a playground.

Our guide was explaining the final step, which was packaging the cubes. I was standing up on my toes, stretching my head over Farid and Abbas to see the labelling machine when my growling stomach alarmed for a couple times.

"Your blood sugar dropped in the sugar factory," Farid grinned.

"We need to eat something soon or I will never organize any other tours!" I told Farid and looked for Babak. Just a few glances around and I found him standing near the exit door at the end of the packing salon.

I approached him. "What do you think about a stopover somewhere to grab a bite on our way back?"

"Are you serious? I'm not sure about it. Boys and girls together?" He seemed a bit surprised.

"Why not? I reckon everybody is hungry. Do you know any places around here?"

"Yes, I do. There are some restaurants on the road to the city. I'll talk with the bus drivers."

I clapped my hands. "Tremendous! And I'll tell the girls about the lunch plan."

The tour inside the factory finished as per the plan and then the shift supervisor guided us to the same spot where we had arrived earlier that morning. We followed the same procedure, the girls got into their own bus and we, the boys, in another one, heading towards the city to have our late lunch.

It was about dusk when we arrived at the university. The students, boys and girls, thanked me for the tour as they got out of the buses. I had a new feeling, something like self-satisfaction leaning towards pride. I was simply happy to finish my very first commitment to the Science Committee.

The sunset added some dark orange colour to the sky while the cold winter wind gently blew off the last remaining dry yellow leaves along University Boulevard.

"Hurry up, man! It's bloody cold," said Farid, rubbing his hands together.

"Just a second," I murmured and approached Taban, who was chatting with Babak and some other guys. "Would you like to come with us?" I asked her, pointing at Farid and myself.

"Oh, thanks, Mr. Zarin. But I have to pass."

A bitter saliva washed down the sweetness of the day as I did not expect that answer. I was about to ask *why* but held my tongue as Babak and a few other guys were staring at us.

VI

A few days later, around lunchtime, I went to the library in the Islamic Theology College to find more references about religious rulings and cleric commandments on music. I had been researching the topic for a long time, and I wanted to wrap it up and publish my article in the Cultural Unit magazine before the end of semester. An old man with a short, white beard sat in front of the entrance, asking students for ID. I passed him, said hello, and waved my hand. He did not ask for my ID and waved back. Entering the salon, I walked directly to the third row at the end. It was an enormous hall with many tables in the centre and Arabic religious phrases from the Quran written on all the walls. An opaque glass wall divided the area into two sections, *Brothers* and *Sisters*. Every single time that I saw those signs, Brothers and Sisters, I asked the same question to myself over and over: *How perverted must be that mindset to separate girls and boys in the public hall of the theology library?* One glance at the bottom shelves and I found the books I had been reading the last few months. A minute later, I sat down at a small table in the Brothers' section. No one was there, so I left the books all over the table and flicked through them. Each of the high-ranked clerics in Iran had an executive directive about music, including listening, singing, playing, or even trading. The deeper I dug, the more I was filled with hatred, disgust, and anger. *Music is not allowed in Islam. Music would cause damage to one's soul. Music is not allowed if it causes temptation. Provocative songs are forbidden, and musical instruments are illegal if they cause sexual desires.* I puffed out a short gloomy sigh after reading each reference. *Who on Earth was following this nonsense? A bunch of sick fanatics, maybe?* I smirked bitterly. Writing down all the quotes, I remembered that I needed to get back to the Science Committee for a meeting about the semester budget's shortfall. Babak had told us we were running out of money for the semester, and he had set up a quick catch-up to discuss it. I gave back the books to the young bookkeeper at the library reception desk and marched back to the Engineering College.

Borhan, Taban, and Anna were sitting around the table when I arrived. A little out of breath, I apologized for the delay and sat next to Taban.

Something was not right. Taban was not smiling, and the others were dead silent. Babak locked the door and leaned against the wall with a piece of paper in his right hand.

I could not resist. "What's happened?"

He showed me the folded paper. "I received this letter from the Islamic Council early this morning. Someone reported our tour. A mixed trip to the sugar factory and a boys-girls gathering afterward in a restaurant out of the city. This is what they've said. They called for the responsible person to be at the Islamic Council office by tomorrow morning at ten o'clock. Basically, this letter is a summons."

I became numb, like a motionless statue for a couple of seconds and my mouth went dry rapidly.

"What? What do you mean?" I asked with a broken voice.

"You signed the separate requests as the committee executive manager. So, you must go there. I don't have any idea what they want," replied Babak, shrugging his shoulders like he had no responsibility.

Borhan chimed in. "Anyway, in these cases, they usually ask some questions about the trip. We haven't done anything wrong or illegal. It was two different tours. We went on separate buses. So, they have nothing against us."

Babak handed the letter to me, unlocked the door, and asked us to get together the next day after I came back from the Islamic Council.

"That's it? Don't you come with me?" I almost shouted.

"Sorry. I'd like to help, but there's nothing I can do. They won't let me in. You should go alone," Babak answered, then left the room.

Taban stared at me, deeply concerned. "Anything I can do?"

I barely smiled and tried not to show any sign of fear. "First, let's see what they want. We'll see tomorrow. Thanks for offering."

I left the room and jogged straight away to the Cultural Unit to find Ali or Saber. The door was partially open. I entered and shut the door tensely. Trying to keep my words calm, I managed to explain the situation and showed them the summons.

Ali pulled a chair over.

"Hey… hey, sit." His hand on my shoulder, he calmly said, "Breathe, buddy."

"What's this shit?" I again showed them the summons.

"Don't worry. They don't do anything. They just want to send a warning to everybody. You didn't organize a party with girls, or serve alcoholic drinks, or traffic drugs. You just went on an educational trip under the permit they had already approved." Ali smirked tensely and then glanced at Saber. "I've been called there several times. Believe me, I know what I'm talking about. This doesn't intend to harm you. It is only to scare the beginners."

Saber handed me a cup of tea. My eyes followed the translucent steam that gradually disappeared before getting anywhere. I exhaled, touched the warmth of the cup's rim with my bottom lip, and leaned back while sipping my tea.

A couple of feeble door knocks took our attention. Ali opened the door.

"Hello, is Mr. Zarin here? May I come in?" It was Taban's voice behind the half-open door.

"Yes, yes please."

I rose from the chair, a bit wobbly as Taban closed the door, eyed on others and came stood in front of me.

"Are you alright Mr. Zarin?" she asked tenderly, gazing at my pale face.

"What can I say?" I tried to show a bit of strength in my voice.

"Would you like me to come with you tomorrow?"

Her words landed on me like the best thing that could happen to me at that moment.

"Umm…" I could not say a word.

Ali came closer and said, "This is very brave of you, Ms. Pakzad. But it's better if you don't show up there." He paused and glanced at me. "It may raise a series of unnecessary questions. You understand me?"

Taban frowned for a split second but soon nodded. "I understand."

I turned to the boys and said, "It would be helpful if one of you could come with me."

"No problem, buddy. See you tomorrow at a quarter to ten o'clock," said Saber without hesitation.

"Seriously? Thanks, man!" I patted Saber's shoulder and glanced at Taban.

She smiled and left the room.

I had a class to attend, but I wasn't in a mood at all. Rushing out of the university, I went to the park. *Everything is going to be fine*, I told myself. *We haven't done anything. They approved our visit and gave us the permits. Are they going for disciplinary action? What if they suspend me from the university? No, no, Ali said it was nothing but a bloody warning trick. He's been there before. It will be alright. I'll be fine.* Struggling to keep the daunting thoughts out of my head, I found myself in front of the telephone centre and instantly an unavoidable need pushed me inside the building. I gave the operator my parents' home phone number and waited near the cabins for my turn. "Mr. Zarin. Cabin five."

That night, I tossed and turned in bed, dragging the moist shrinking linen under my pillow. I woke up several times before dawn, when I decided to get out of bed before the alarm went off. I could barely see anything inside the room. Rubbing my eyes, I touched the wall and found the light switch. Sharp yellow light stung my eyes like a needle, forcing my eyelids lower. My head felt heavier, pushing me to sit on the edge of the bed for a minute or more till the pressure lifted from my neck. Leaving the room slowly, I washed my face in the sink in silence as I was trying not to make loud noises and wake up Farid. A few minutes later, I came back to my room. Things were clearer! Looking for appropriate clothes to wear, I chose my plain blue shirt from the small closet near the bed and tried it on. I paired it with my jeans, but everybody knew that wearing jeans was not a wise option when one was called to the Islamic Council. They would always interpret it as a sort of symbol of Western culture. So, I changed into a pair of loose black cotton trousers.

As I was getting ready to sneak out, I practiced what to say and how to explain the tour in front of whoever was supposed to question me. I grabbed my backpack from the floor behind the door, then thought better of it, due to the same reason that I didn't wear my jeans. Unzipping the backpack, I took out the research draft about music versus cleric commandments and left it on the bedside table. After a short pause, I also left the backpack on the bed, sneaked out of my room, and headed to the university while Farid was still sleeping.

I rubbed my hands and blew a warm breath out to see if any cloud would form in front of my eyes or not. A tiny white cloud flew away in haste. I put my hands in my jacket pockets and walked to Abad Boulevard to take a cab. The grey sky seemed darker than normal. Faded, misty, tawny clouds around streetlight bulbs shivered in the occasional howling wind. I turned my head down for a moment, staring at the pedestrian way covered under dirty, frosty broken leaves.

There weren't many cars on the streets at that time, but I found a cab easily. The driver was an old man with small eyes and an unshaven face.

"Just finished my work. Heading back home now. Where are you coming from, son? Tehran?" he asked me with a raspy voice a few seconds after I had got in.

I was not in a mood to talk at all. "Yes," I answered unenthusiastically.

He didn't look at me, but continued, "Student? Grand State University?"

I stared at the tiny, uniform mist layer on the window. "Yes," was my short answer that came out irritably.

He glanced at me through the rear-view mirror. "You don't live in a dorm, son, do you?"

I was nervous and the old driver kept asking me questions. "No, I do not."

He might have only been trying to have a friendly chitchat after his long night shift, but it was annoying. So annoying that I imagined I was in a mobile interrogation cell. I had no choice but to ask him to pull over before losing my temper.

I wandered a bit down University Boulevard, then headed to the Engineering College café. I was the first costumer. The young owner had just turned on the heaters around the café. Warming up my nose with both hands, I ordered a cup of tea and sat on the bench near a small electrical heater beside the cashier, gazing at the sweltering-red coils, and tried not to think about anything.

I couldn't realize how much time had passed by as the café was getting crowded fast, and a familiar pop song from the radio reminded me of the day before when I had been reading different clerics' commandments about music.

"Good morning," Saber said. He was standing near the table holding a plastic tray in his hands. Scattered laughter from a queue of three or four students near the cashier and some other guys in front of the heater distracted Saber for a second. He put the tray on the table and sat in front of me. "Oh man, you look terrible! Had a rough night?" he murmured, nibbling on fried eggs. "Have you had your breakfast? Dig in."

"I'm fine. Thanks, can't eat anything now. A bit worried about today."

"Where is Babak? He's the science committee leader, for god's sake!"

"Beats me. Haven't seen him since yesterday morning."

Saber didn't say anything; he shook his head and gulped his next bite.

"How well do you know Babak?" I asked Saber on our way to the Islamic Council.

"Not much. He's a friend of Jalal. They came from the same city. Why do you ask?"

"Nothing. Just asking."

The Islamic Council was a two-story building with a yellow brick exterior façade. A temporary photo exhibition from the Iran Islamic Revolution was going on in the lobby. Iran had a monarchy prior to the Islamic Revolution. The anniversary events for the Islamic Revolution were about to start in a couple of weeks and all government organizations were preparing themselves for the celebration. Black and white pictures from more than twenty years back were hanging everywhere, on the walls or from loose exhibition stands. A poor-quality replica of a newspaper from those days at the end of the exhibition caught my eyes. *The Shah Is Gone* was the most famous headline, printed in bold large fonts on the front page among some black and white photos. It meant the king of Iran left the country forever. After glancing at the photos, we walked to the administration room.

It was a tiny room, the walls painted a faded green colour and a side grey door to another section. The receptionist was a young boy with freshly grown facial hair, more like a teenager than a mature university staff, and I wondered if maybe he was one of the university students, too. I showed him the summons and asked what to do. He glanced at the paper, and then stared at us like he was the most important person in the entire university. Then he bent his head down to some papers in front of him and began flicking them as slowly as any ignorant person could do. I was pretty sure he was not reading or even searching for anything. Some seconds later, he glanced at us, pointed to the small grey door on his left, and said, "Mr. Haji is busy now. But you can go in. Only you. Not you!" He asked Saber to wait outside.

Saber glanced at me, smiled, patted my back, and left the reception area. I knocked and entered the room with a grey door. Two guys sat around an old wooden table and a middle-aged man with a long, curly beard, enough to cover his neck, was standing near the open window. He was wearing a white shirt, untucked, on top of his bleached brown army-style pants, with all the buttons fastened up to his neck. A big silver ring with a dark red agate stone covered one-third of his right ring finger. A prayer bump on his forehead seemed like a burning wound, same size as a walnut. It was frightening, not because it gave him a monstrous appearance, but due to the terrifying concept behind it. It was like a gang tattoo on his forehead to show off his ultimate devotion to religious rituals, specifically, too much praying every day. My eyes fixed on the horrifying prayer bump and my lips tightened. He did not have any shoes on, but instead, wore a pair of black slippers. I detested him on the spot and guessed that he must be Mr. Haji. His first impression with me was awfully disgusting, so I had not paid any attention to the other guys in the room.

I reluctantly introduced myself, showing the letter and waiting in front of the door.

He asked me to sit down, calmly walked to a metal filing cabinet near his desk and fumbled for something. The other guys left the room from the same door I had come in.

The man took out a yellow folder from the top drawer and approached the table. "Do you want tea?" he asked me without looking at me, and kept himself busy flipping some papers around in the folder.

"No, thanks, Mr. Haji."

He poured a cup of tea from a metallic flask on his messy desk and sat in front of the table, opposite me. "Mr. Zarin! You were in charge of last week's factory tour. How did it go?" he asked me in a low tone, while he put a corner of a sugar cube in his cup, soaked it with tea, then started slurping it.

"It was a very useful scientific site visit, Mr. Haji. Um… it went per plan. The shift supervisor's assistant led us to every section of the factory and explained the process. Um… we learned a lot." I felt like I was talking a bit of nonsense.

"How was the after-party in the restaurant?" he spat out.

"Sorry? Say that again, please," I asked hesitantly.

"We've been informed that a bunch of girls and boys travelled to the factory and then headed to a restaurant together without university permission, thereby breaching Islamic rules by wearing inappropriate clothes and behaving inappropriately." He stared at me, waiting for my answer.

"No, Mr. Haji. No Islamic rules have been broken. Believe me." I paused for a second and cautiously added, "Mr. Haji, I didn't realise that we needed a permit to go to lunch. I thought the consent was required only for the factory visit."

He did not say anything for a couple of seconds and just kept looking at the folder. Caressing his beard, he raised his voice. "As long as you are a student at the university, you need permits for everything, unless you don't want to continue your education!"

My eyes crawled from his hidden mouth inside the messy beard to the creepy prayer bump on his forehead and my lips squeezed together. The more he talked, the angrier and more confused I was.

"Open both your ears very carefully and listen. This situation needs formal action. I will act upon our regulations and send a notice of suspension for this semester to the Dean, as you were the tour organizer," he murmured, thumbing the folder carelessly.

I was not sure if he was threatening me, bluffing, or if he was serious about taking formal action. I was frozen like a tiny, fragile icicle hanging from the roof gutter. I had to make up my mind and say something before melting down and getting crushed to a thousand pieces.

He continued, "So, it's up to you now. I can treat this meeting as a formal warning to you, close my eyes on this unethical behaviour, and stop this trouble right here, in this room, without issuing any suspension notice if you tell me what happened during the tour and afterward in the restaurant?"

My hands clenched into fists for a moment, and I began shaking my feet under the table without noticing it. His patronizing gesture was hideous. "Mr. Haji, we just had a late lunch. Everybody was starving, and we agreed to have something on our way back. Believe me."

"We? Who is this 'we'?" He stared into my eyes and fidgeted with his red agate ring.

I stopped talking for a moment to figure out if it was right to bring up any name or not. "Me and the Science Committee leader."

Mr. Haji did not react to my answer, neither a sign of belief nor disbelief.

"Tell me why girls were sitting among boys at the same table and chatting without full Islamic hijab? Where the hell did you think you were? Overseas? Western countries?" he almost shouted.

I was baffled and frightened. "Um… we were not together. It wasn't the same table. Girls were sitting separately from boys with full hijab," I muttered.

"That's enough. I'll record a formal warning in your Islamic Ethical Behaviour folder. It means if something like this happens again, you will face at least one semester suspension from the university. You can go now."

He looked down and began to busy himself writing something in the yellow folder.

I did not understand what had just happened. I did not say anything, I just stood up and left the room out of sheer strength.

Saber was still sitting on a scratched-up bench in the salon.

I was shaking, and my hands were still clenched in fists. Muttering in broken phrases, I managed to explain what had happened inside.

Patting my back, he said, "You see?! It was nothing to be worried about. He just wanted to scare you."

My eyes grew wide as if I couldn't figure out his words. "But he wrote a notice in my Islamic Ethical Behaviour folder and will send a formal notice to the Dean. Next time, they will suspend me for the entire semester."

"Oh, come on. Don't worry, buddy. There is no rule anywhere in the university system that boys and girls cannot go to restaurants together. They have nothing against you. This is the famous dirty trick to scare new students and ask them to rat on others, most of the time with threats and seldom giving them opportunities."

"You reckon?"

Saber paused for a second, glanced around and whispered, "Yes."

CHAPTER 5

I

t was mid-February or a bit later when Saber told me the Islamic Council had rejected my article on music and did not issue the permit to publish it in the Cultural Unit journal.

"It was obvious, buddy. What else did you expect?" asked Saber without expecting any answer.

Karim later explained that the topic was terribly sensitive and could raise unnecessary attention followed by excessive tension. "Chasing this one is not an option, buddy! Let it go."

I didn't resubmit my research for the second review and eventually, it ended up in the bin. Maybe because I was afraid of possible consequences or simply because I was overwhelmed by tonnes of other things around me.

A few days later, Babak told me he had sorted out the Science Committee financial concern and a limited amount of money was made available to print out the new revision of the committee's journal. We didn't want more delay as the Iranian new year holidays would start mid-March onward. Everybody would get busy with the new year celebration and would be leaving the university for almost two weeks.

"Splendid! How did you do it?" I asked Babak while he was writing something on a piece of paper.

He turned back, tucked the corner of his plain olive shirt into his pants and handed me the paper. Glancing at me, he rapidly took an open, half-filled envelope from the table and threw it in his bag. I couldn't see what it was inside the envelope, but it looked like cash notes. "Dr. Saraf, our beloved thermodynamics professor, kindly supported us by donating money to the committee and I gathered the rest from different sources." He smiled and adjusted his glasses on his nose. "This is the address of the publisher with whom we usually handle our works. It is a small office not far from Shahid Boulevard. Make sure all copies are being printed in high quality and binding is accurate. I've already talked with the publishing house manager. His name is Javad, and he's aware that you'll be there." Babak then explained the printing process step by step as I was new to the job.

"Okay. Got it!" I replied with confidence and asked him if the final edit was ready.

"Taban is aware of it. She promised that it would be ready by tomorrow. I gotta go now." He grabbed his bag and rushed to the door. "Oh, one more thing—don't worry about the payment. See you later, buddy."

Babak left the room while I stood there with a gigantic question mark over my head. *Taban? Has he just called Miss Pakzad by her first name?* It was weirdly unorthodox as all boys used to call girls by their surnames, and he just called Miss Pakzad by her first name, Taban, in a casual way. *Why did he say Taban and not Miss Pakzad this time?* was the only question in my head. That was the first time I had heard Babak called Taban by her first name. I was baffled and annoyed. Struggling not to speculate, I thought to myself, *Are they friends? Close together? No. No. They are not. The physics class will start soon, and I'll see Taban in the classroom. Then I'll ask her about the final edit. No more thinking of Babak.*

With the publishing office address in my hand, I left the room and rushed to the classroom. The professor came in earlier than usual and I did not have a chance to talk with Taban. The professor started the session with a review of the previous lessons, talking about how to calculate the amount of carried out work. Taban was sitting near me, but in the left section of the classroom. I turned a bit to the left and glanced at Taban. She didn't catch my glimpse, though. Trying to forget about the first name-surname dilemma, I shifted my thoughts to publishing the journal as the professor continued his tutorial. A few minutes later came the impulsive second try, but successfully. Catching her eye, I voicelessly told Taban to stay in the classroom after the lecture, so we could talk about the magazine. She nodded her head in agreement, smiled and gazed back at the green chalkboard.

The professor was a young woman, speaking monotonously in low pitch, making it more difficult for me to focus. "Imagine a soccer ball on top of this building. It has a potential energy of the elevation of the building multiplied by the gravity. Drop the ball and you release the stored energy." She was simultaneously explaining static and kinetic energy correlations and writing the conversion formula on the green chalkboard.

Farid arrived at class a bit late, sat near me, and poked my hip with his pen.

"Amin invited us to his place this afternoon," said Farid.

"Cool. What time?"

"Seven-ish. Ali and Jalal will be coming, too," Farid replied without looking at me.

"Nice. I'll be back before six o'clock and we'll go there together."

I was looking at the chalkboard pretending to listen to the lecture. The professor finished the lecture and asked the last person to erase the filled-up board. She left the classroom while we continued to copy the board.

"Are you joining us for lunch, or what? Abbas and Reza are waiting outside," Farid asked me.

"I'll join you later," was my quick response.

Farid glanced at Taban and whispered in my ear, "Why don't you ask Miss Pakzad to come over this evening? We'll all go to Amin's house together."

He grinned and joined the other fellows while Taban was talking with other girls near the podium. She looked over at me after I finished chatting with Farid.

"Miss Pakzad. Do you have a moment?" I asked her in front of the other girls, which caused a moment of short pause among them.

"Yes, sure."

She had expected the question, said goodbye to her friends, and we left the classroom. Walking towards the Science Committee, I glanced at her thick, bright, ruby lips and said, "Babak told me that you are about to complete the final edit?"

"Yes. He asked me the other day to proof-check it again for the last time."

We arrived at the committee room. I pushed the door open for her, and we entered. I deliberately left the door open and said, "I was under the impression that Babak was going to proofread it."

"Me too, but he asked me just a couple days ago. That's fine. I've almost finished it. It will be all set by tonight. Are you going to the printing office tomorrow?"

I felt a bit muddled as I had not told her about my plan or the publisher. *How did she know about it? Babak just told me a couple hours ago. How did she figure out that Babak got the money and resolved the financial problem?* "What? How did you know my plan?" I asked in bewilderment.

"I'm the admin manager, Mr. Zarin! It means I know everything," she replied with a spark of teasing in her charming smile.

"Indeed, you are! Of course, you do!"

A few minutes later, Borhan and another member of the committee entered the room. I told them that the financial issues had been sorted out, and we would print out the journals soon. Then I started explaining the importance of advertisement to the successful distribution of the magazines. "They'll be ready shortly, a couple days or three at the most, and we have to let everybody know about it right now. I reckon we are running out of time."

We discussed our strategy for about half an hour. Taban winked at me and said she had to go to the canteen for lunch as her friends were waiting. I truly liked when she winked at me or using her eyes to signal something. I wrapped up the unplanned meeting and followed her while Borhan and the other guy stayed in the room. After we walked out of the building, a man in the corridor asked her if Babak was in the room. His face was familiar, but I could not recall him. Taban smiled and responded that he might be in the library.

"Do you know him?" I asked Taban.

"Yes, he's Babak's roommate in the dorm."

"Wow, you know everybody. How do you know Babak's pal?" I asked in a friendly tone.

"Mr. Zarin. I told you. I'm the admin manager. This is my job to know people."

We chuckled as we passed the amphitheatre.

"Can I say something?" Taban asked softly, looking at me with her serene shiny eyes.

"Yes, sure. What is it? Is it about Babak?" I regretted the words the moment I spit Babak's name out.

"Yes." She paused. "The other day, he asked me about the way we are hanging out together, you and me. He knew we sometimes walk back to our apartments together. It is not important at all, but he asked me to be more cautious. Anyway, I told him off and made it clear that my relationship was none of his business. Mr. Zarin, I just want you to be aware that this conversation happened between me and him."

My mouth shut, my eyes widened, and I got goosebumps over my arms. In my mind, I repeated what she had just told me and tried to be sure that I had heard her correctly as I had not expected that dialogue at all. Trying to digest her words, I said, "Oh, of course. What a patronizing gesture! Not cool. It's not anyone's business to tell you what to do or how to do it." The words came out of my mouth quite banal as I did not know what else to say. I was suspended in a void without a clue if she was into me or something else.

A few minutes later, we arrived at the canteen. Taban assured me that she would bring the file the next morning.

After she left, I waited at the restaurant for some minutes, thinking about what I had just heard. *What did she mean? Why did she share it with me?*

II

It was about seven o'clock in the evening when Farid and I arrived at Amin's house. He lived with his parents in a classic-style, two-story building with a cosy backyard which was impressively planted with roses and three chubby orange trees. I was pretty sure a professional gardener took care of that flawless backyard.

Ali and Jalal were already there. Amin greeted us cheerfully and turned on the backyard lighting. It wasn't the first time we had met him at his house, so we knew our way in. The guest hall was separated from the TV room, but we usually sat on a comfortable sofa in the TV room where two amber wall lights gave the room a super warm vibe.

"Want a tea or coffee?" Amin asked everybody while trying to find the TV remote control. "Yup! Found it!" He gave the remote control to Jalal and headed to the kitchen.

I followed Amin to the kitchen to give him a hand. Leftover pilaf on a round plate under a glass dome lid on the dining table caught my eyes. I removed the lid and nibbled on a bit.

"Are you hungry? Let me order pizza now," he said while pouring tea in transparent glasses.

"No, thanks. Just wanted to try that traditional crispy rice. Delish! Any news?" I put the lid back, passed him two clean cups from the table, and placed a crystal bowl of sugar cubes on a silver tea tray.

"News? There is always something happening in this country. Wait for it." He took the tray, and we went back to the room. The TV was on satellite channel, BBC World News. Satellite TV was illegal in Iran, but almost everybody had it.

"What's up, guys? Update me!" I shouted while patting Ali's shoulder and trying to squeeze myself on the sofa between him and Jalal. "Give me some room!"

Amin said, "Ali was talking about another student movement in Tehran before you arrived."

Ali sipped his hot tea. "Some universities have recently initiated a new protest against the totalitarian approach in the academic system. It started last week following the activist student's expulsion. The authorities later released a note that they had found him guilty of sedition, but they didn't publish any further details."

Jalal turned the TV volume down. "They were also leading a campaign for freedom of speech. The campaign took lots of attention outside of the university."

Ali was opening a delicate topic and expanding it cautiously. Somehow, it gave me the impression that he was going to request something. He continued, "Everyone knows that the Basij Organization is linked to the Islamic Council and the Council is reporting to the Ministry of Intelligence. In this case, students in the Basij Organization do not take orders from the university even though it is categorized as a student association."

Amin asked, "What's next? What is happening now?"

Ali scratched his forehead. "Saber is currently in an urgent meeting with our friends from different colleges. We've been informed that students in other cities, such as Isfahan and Tabriz, are going to join the Tehran protest. They are enormous cities, and their support gives more power to the Tehran protest. Saber is now planning how and when to unite with the movement." Ali paused like he forgot the proper words, then cleared his throat and continued. "We must not stay silent. We do not want to go back to those years when the Basij Organization had control all over the university, and we are aiming to make them purely a student organization, not a governmental spy agency."

A few minutes later, Farid cracked a short joke, interrupted the whole conversation, and stood up. "Guys, enough politics. Let's have dinner! I'm starving."

"Good idea!" Amin shouted.

Farid was rapidly switching TV channels to find a music or dance show. He was still a bit down from his breakup with Asal. Apparently, her father had decided to transfer Asal to another college near their hometown.

I followed Farid's suggestion. "No more politics! Let's play cards after dinner!"

Amin ordered pizzas via phone while I cleaned up the coffee table and Ali took care of the empty cups.

"How's it going with the Science Committee's magazine? Jalal told me the financial problem is all cleared up," Ali asked me on his way to the kitchen with the silver tray in his hands.

I stared at him, surprised. Jalal grinned. "How on Earth do you know that? I was just told about it before coming here!" I almost yelled at Jalal while looking back at Ali, who had just stepped out of the kitchen.

Jalal could not resist laughing. "We know everything."

"Shut up! Tell me!"

"Babak told me almost two days ago."

I shook my head in disbelief. "What the hell? He just told me today. And why did he tell *you*?"

Ali couldn't stop chuckling. "Did you forget Babak and Jalal are friends from the same city?"

Jalal added, "Our common friend came over from our hometown for a couple days, and Babak asked me to join them for dinner. We talked about various things, and he told me that Miss Pakzad gave him ten thousand to publish the journal. He was head over heels. Apparently, the money was more than enough."

My smile dissipated and at the same time thick wrinkles formed in my forehead. Something like a blistering flash fire moved over my body. "What? What do you mean Miss Pakzad gave him ten thousand? That's a lot of money. How come?"

"Miss Pakzad and Babak are friends. So, she helped him to handle the financial problem. Babak promised to give her all her money back after selling the journals."

I could not believe what I had just heard.

Farid observed the spasm in my face, stopped watching TV, came near me, and asked Jalal, "Are you sure that they are *friends*?"

"Yes, I'm positive. Babak has hit on her from the very beginning. They often go out together. I saw them myself several times in different cafés and restaurants."

Farid gazed at me, but did not say anything.

I couldn't gather my thoughts. I tried to say something but was utterly shocked. I could not even swallow.

"What's the problem?" Ali asked while approaching me.

Farid again glanced at me and smoothly answered, "Nima has feelings for Miss Pakzad."

I interrupted Farid. "But how is it possible? She didn't say anything to me about Babak. I'm sure she likes me, too. We were often hanging around together, chatting for a long time. I'm sure of it. She showed interest in me, too." I was out of control and pathetically repeating myself.

Jalal glanced at Ali and Amin, then me. "Are you sure? How do you know? Because I'm certain that they are together."

I was emotionally drained, but managed to control myself. Trying to keep calm, I answered, "I'm positive. She likes me. Don't know how to explain it. I have no doubt." I sank on the sofa and started to tap my fingers on my knees.

Amin hesitantly looked at me. "Some girls aim to catch up with several boys for different reasons. Maybe Miss Pakzad likes you as an active, interesting boy, and she likes hanging out with Babak because he's in his last year of uni, has lots of experience, and many connections everywhere."

I did not want to accept it, although it was a reasonable argument. "I can't believe it. I have to find out the truth." I asked Jalal not to bring up this conversation with Babak. "Please, please do not tell anyone about it till I figure this shit out."

Jalal sat near me and calmly smiled. "Not a problem, buddy. Don't worry about it. Good luck!"

III

I didn't want to think about it but couldn't avoid it. Picturing Taban and Babak together at their favourite restaurant, I rolled on my bed, trying to keep my eyes shut and forget everything. The feverish dream made my night tormenting as Taban and Babak were all over it. They were talking about final exams, and Taban was laughing at Babak's jokes while he handed her a piece of pizza. It wasn't all. They were walking along the University Boulevard and waving to our classmates.

Finally, the alarm from the small clock on the bedside table went off and ended my miserable night. I stretched my hand and turned off the alarm. Rubbing my eyes, I got out of the bed, turned on the light, and sluggishly got ready.

How's it better to react when I see Taban? Should I bring up anything about Babak? Or better to be cold with her? Maybe ask her to tell me everything? were the thoughts swirling in my head on my way to the university.

The college's foyer was crowded as everybody was rushing to their classes. Nodding my head to familiar faces, I passed by them fast and I found myself in front of the Science Committee room. There they were, Taban and Babak, standing near the computer desk chatting quietly. I froze for a couple seconds, choked again by the invisible lump of cold tar sticking in my throat.

I turned around, trying to avoid eye contact, and began to leave the room.

"Good morning, Nima. Just in time! Come on in," Babak shouted as he approached the door. We shook hands as a usual way to say hello, and he passed me a three-inch floppy disk in a transparent, plastic hard cover labelled, *S.C. Magazine, Ready to print*. I recognized Taban's handwriting—all letters were the same size, slanted and in one straight line.

I tried to act normal.

"Good on you. I'll take it from here." Then I glanced at Taban.

"Thanks, pal. I have a tutorial to attend. I hope the magazines will be ready by tomorrow," said Babak. He waved his right hand, adjusted his grey suit collar, and left the room.

I stared at Taban and waited for a few seconds as she might be telling me everything about her friendship with Babak, but nothing happened. *Is she ignoring me?*

"I thought *you* were supposed to give this to me?" I asked with a trembling hand as I held up the floppy disk to Taban.

She turned off the computer and smiled, like everything was alright. "Oh, yes. I came earlier to make another copy of the floppy disk. When I finished it, I left the copied disk near the computer and stuck a label on it for you. Mr. Asgari was just passing. He saw me here and stopped by. As soon as he took the disk from the desk, you showed up. That is why he handed over it to you." Taban then grabbed her purse, smiled again and continued, "Come on, Mr. Zarin. We have electrical engineering course in five minutes. Let's go."

On one hand, her story made sense, and everything was fine, but on the other hand, I couldn't erase my mind from what I heard last night. It hurt to think about being played by Babak and Taban. It was an unpleasant outburst of jealousy and foolishness combined with torturous reflections of being deceived and manipulated. I had never had such a feeling in my life, and it wasn't easy to handle.

"Are you okay? Is everything alright?" Taban asked me, standing near the Science Committee door, waiting for me. Her voice softly floated towards me.

"Yes. Fine. Let's go." I couldn't open up.

Taban stared at me all the way to the class. "What's happened here?" she asked in the staircase to the second floor.

"Nothing, Miss Pakzad. I'm fine," I answered, avoiding eye contact with her as I pushed the door open for her.

We sat in the same seats as usual.

"Did I do something wrong? Why did you become quiet all of a sudden?" Taban whispered and leaned forward toward my seat.

"Not at all. I'm fine. Just thinking about something." I wanted to say, *or someone,* but I had to bite my tongue as the professor showed up at the door.

Taban was one row behind my seat, and I couldn't see her, but I sensed that she was staring at me. My eyes followed the professor's hand as it moved randomly from the top to the bottom of the board, but I couldn't pay attention at all. *Jalal is Babak's friend. He told me that Babak would never work for free.* This had been continuously ringing a bell in my mind since last night. Rumour had it that the Science Committee was a small business for Babak, but I had always ignored those scattered stories till the night before. *How did he convince Taban to give him money? He received funds from the uni. Dr. Saraf also financially supported the magazine. So why did Babak ask for cash from Taban? Why did Taban give him the money and did not say anything to me?*

I turned my notebook to the last page and began to write down all the expenses for the year as far as I could remember. I was organizing everything in the Committee, so I was roughly aware of some incomes and expenditures. I didn't know the exact sum but had a ballpark figure. The sugar factory tour, software instructors for training courses, the magazine... Listing them, I realized that none of the committee's members—except Babak—had a clear idea of incoming funds. I wasn't able to estimate how much cash Babak got from different sources. *Is it possible that he received money from other sponsors? What about advertisements? He printed two ads in the magazine last semester, one from a local bookshop and the other from an institute of foreign languages. He told us they often help the Committee, and it was fine to publish their ads free of charge.*

I scratched my forehead. "Bullshit!" was my thought that wrongly came out of my mouth instead of fading inside my head.

Farid poked me hard. "What's wrong with you today? Shut up!"

The professor stopped writing and turned back to the students. Luckily, he hadn't understood what had slipped out of my mouth and continued to fill the chalkboard with a tediously boring formula about calculating heat loss due to resistance in a simple electrical network.

I stared at the expenses list again. *Something is wrong,* was my logical conclusion and *something must be wrong!* was my hope.

Rattling thoughts inside my head made it difficult for me to stay in the class any longer. "I'm gonna go to the publishing office." I hurriedly gave Farid a heads-up and knocked off while the professor was still facing the chalkboard.

Outside of the room was so quiet as no one was on the floor. *Now it's a good time to do it.* An idea popped in my head and led me to the Science Committee room. I locked the door behind myself, paused near the table and watched around as I did not know what exactly I was looking for. Pulling out all drawers, I fumbled through different folders, looked inside envelopes, reopened unsealed boxes, and even scanned sticky notes. Tapping on the floor with my foot, I gave up and sat behind the computer desk. *How's it possible? Not a single receipt or any record from financial transactions. It doesn't make any sense, or does it?* I double checked if everything was in the same place as before and headed straight away to the printing office.

I took out a crumbled paper from my pocket and checked the address while I was walking fast along University Boulevard. Babak had told me not to be worried about the payment. *Babak said that he took care of everything. He is up to something. No doubt about it! I need something to prove it. I have to collect evidence as much as I can. Even one tiny shred of proof!*

An old, dirty yellow cab with a broken headlight honked a couple of times and stopped after I waved my hand.

"Are you going to the end of Shahid Boulevard?" I asked the tan-faced driver, and he nodded his head.

It wasn't an easy task to find a clean spot in the backseat. Zigzagging among the other cars, the driver overtook them and then triumphantly eyeballed the other drivers in the street. Dancing particles of dust in the sunlight inside the cab distracted me for a few moments, but just for some seconds, not more, as I was again surrounded by the inciting thoughts of gathering evidence against Babak.

"This is the end of the Shahid Boulevard. Getting out here or heading farther?" said the driver in a low tone and pulled over as I quickly paid the fare and got out of the stinky cab.

It was almost lunchtime. Roaring cars were clumsily circling around the roundabout at the end of the boulevard and honking frequently while motorcycles with two or sometimes three passengers randomly filled the tiny gaps between the cars. I eyed around several times and hardly spotted the publishing office's neon-lit sign on the other side of the roundabout, just in front of the crammed street. A traffic light and zebra crossing were a bit farther, but I didn't bother and instead found shortcuts between the moving cars and the storming motorcycles. A thick dark plume puffed out of the rusted exhaust pipe underneath of an old Mercedes minibus, while a chubby man behind the role tried to park that mini smoke factory in front of the printing office. Waving my hands, I tried to inhale anything but the burning diesel fumes. I jumped over a narrow water channel between the street and the pedestrian way and almost collided with a group of men in formal suits who were partially blocking the pedestrian way, talking. An old man with a tiny hunch on his back was smoking near his grocery shop. He was struggling to move two boxes of glass Coca Cola bottles with his right foot to the entrance. I passed him, strode towards the blinking red neon sign, and entered the publishing office.

The place smelled like plastic doll or liquid glue. It was a small shop with more than a few photocopy machines and a couple of plotters at the end of the salon.

"Hello. How are you today? My name is Nima, from Grand State Uni. Babak's friend."

"Good day. I'm Javad. I was expecting you." He was a short, skinny man in his fifties with a long black moustache.

"I brought you the final file for printing," I said while trying to find the floppy disk in my backpack.

"Yes. Your friend, Babak, was here yesterday. He told my son, Hamid, that you'd bring the file today. I booked you one of our machines for this afternoon. I'll ask Hamid to finish the printing by tonight and we'll sort out the cover tomorrow."

"That would be great! Thanks."

I handed him the floppy disk while thinking about expenses. Scratching my head, I turned around. No customer was there at that time. I mumbled a bit to buy more time and make up my mind about whether or not to ask anything about Babak and the financial part of that order.

I kept a stupid smile on my face and awkwardly said, "Um…was Babak here yesterday? Why?" I regretted it the moment I asked.

"Yes, he was. He settled up the bill."

Javad inserted the floppy into the computer's disk drive. I couldn't see any signs of suspicion in his behaviour. I needed to have more information about expenses. *This could be a perfect opportunity*. I did not want to raise any attention to the subject. Most crucially, I knew that Babak had been working with them for the past couple of years. *What if they tell Babak I was up to something? What if they are close friends? I have to do something fast.*

"Yes, yes. He'd told me about it. Is Hamid here today?" was my next move.

"No, he'll be back this evening."

This was the perfect moment. Suddenly, an idea enlightened me like I found the key to decode that mystery. *It is a bit risky but worth a shot!*

I tried to act normal by looking around, pretending to get bored, and trying to chat about anything that came to mind. "I hope we can sell our magazines fast. We need that money for the Science Committee."

"Don't worry, son. You'll do."

"You know, it was difficult for us to gather all the required money to print the magazine. I'm very happy that we finally did it. By the way, has Babak paid it all?"

"Yes. Hamid told me he received the full payment. He often takes care of bills. I hope our special discount for students helped a bit."

I got goosebumps. I was putting my words in order and almost shouted, "Oh, yes, I know. Babak briefly told me yesterday. By the way, it seems he forgot the receipt. Um…" I froze for a split-second but managed to put my words together. "I'm wondering if you could make me a copy. We need it for record keeping." I held my breath unintentionally for a couple of seconds, worried it had not worked.

"Not a problem, son. Let me finish transferring your file to the computer, and I'll sort that out as well," he answered calmly as if that was not an unusual request. His reaction thawed my cold feet. "Oh, come on," he said to the computer. "Faster. Yes, finished!" Finally done, he headed to the cashier desk. I could feel my heart beating in my chest. He unlocked a drawer and brought out a brown A3-size payment tracking logbook. He flipped through the pages, looking for the transaction record. "Yesterday? Yesterday? Yes! Found it. Just a moment." He took out a small receipt notebook from another drawer, laid a blue carbon sheet between two pages, and wrote the expenses in four or five lines. "There you go!" He tore the perforated upper section, stamped and signed it, placed the original receipt in a white envelope, and handed it over to me while keeping the carbon copy for himself.

I shivered a bit, got goosebumps again and started tapping the floor with the tip of foot nervously. I accepted the envelope with a shaking hand. "Thank you so much, Mr. Javad!"

Leaving the store, I could not wait to see the contents, but didn't want to look at the receipt in front of the shop as I felt like I had stolen something. Walking faster than usual for about ten minutes, I found myself near a restaurant where mostly construction workers ate lunch. I entered, ordered my lunch over the counter, sat down behind a long table, and opened the envelope.

Printing: 3,400 Toman
Cover and bond: 500 Toman
Grand total: 3,900 Toman.
Including 20% Special Student's Discount. Tax included.

"Oh, my goodness!" I almost shouted. The gap between the total cost of the magazine and the cash he received from Taban was a considerable amount of money for college students. Let aside additional funds that he had taken from the other sponsors. I smiled diabolically, filled with comforting aura of success combined with a dash of resentment. *I was bloody right.* Trying to recall how much Babak told me that magazine printing costs, I checked the receipt for the fourth time.

"Is this your order? Chicken with rice?" A young guy in a stained white apron was holding a big plate in his hand and staring at me.

"Yes. Thanks."

He left the plate at the table without looking at me and moved to the next table to take the dirty dishes. Suddenly starving, I took a deep breath, inhaling the smell of the white rice that looked like a small hill surrounded by steaming clouds. It had a touch of eye-catching yellow saffron on top, garnished by pan-seared barberries with a juicy chicken thigh. Knowing I needed to eat, I put the receipt in the envelope and placed it in my backpack, but it could not stop me from thinking. *What should I do now? Babak is not my friend, but he is not a bad person. Um... but he took money from Taban and deceived all of us. Taban must know. Babak does not deserve her.*

I finished my lunch and headed to the dormitory. Daylight was gradually fading behind the thick blanket of grey clouds.

Sitting in a cab and drawing parallel lines on the misty window with my index finger, I hoped that Ali or Jalal could help me somehow.

It was about three o'clock when I arrived. I didn't knock and opened the door soundlessly. Ali was wearing brown-hatched pyjamas, lying on his bed and reading a book, while Jalal was behind a small desk studying for final exams.

"My sincere apology for interrupting your awfully boring afternoon. I need your help!" I shouted, keeping a cheeky grin on my face.

"What the heck are you doing here?" Ali said loudly.

Jalal burst out with laughter.

I cleared my throat. "Guys, guys, come on. I need to talk with you about something important."

I locked the door and found a clean mug near the window. Pouring tea from the electric kettle near Ali's bed, I explained the mismatch between payment to the publishing office and the amount that Babak had gathered and claimed. They listened carefully without interjecting.

When I finished, Jalal said, "Nima, are you sure? This is a significant accusation."

"It happened. He did it. I have the proof."

I glanced at Ali, seeking his endorsement. He said, "Yes. It is almost obvious that he's cheating the system. And you got him very well."

"So, what should I do now? On one hand, I don't want to create a nasty mess, but on the other hand, I cannot keep my mouth shut and ignore it."

"Is it about you and Miss Pakzad?" Jalal asked me cautiously.

"Does it matter?" I answered after a momentary pause.

Ali approached me, then looked at Jalal. "When is Babak going to graduate?"

"It must be his last semester. He'll probably defend his thesis before summer holidays," answered Jalal.

"There we go—his last term. Can you manage it without a scandal?"

I sipped my tea, put the half-full mug on the bedside table, and slowly clapped my hands. "You are a genius! Come on, man. Use your brain. This is why I'm here now. I need to find a painless way to sort this shit out. My question is *how*?"

Jalal could not stop laughing.

I continued, "I don't want to tell him myself directly. Um… I was thinking about bringing up this issue with the other committee members and asking for something like an impeachment."

Jalal thought a bit. "Listen, Nima, that's not a bad idea, but it might be better not to call it an impeachment. Try to sort it out in another way. Um… I don't know, maybe a retirement? I'm not saying this because he is my friend. Remember that he'll be leaving the uni soon, anyway. He did many things for the committee. I'm aware that he didn't do it for free, but he worked very well for students."

"Good idea, pal! Sounds like a plan. I'll think about it tonight."

"More tea? With honey? Local honey from the east mountain," Ali said, showing me the amber-coloured jar.

"No, thanks. I have to go. Need to sort out this issue." I stood up to leave the room.

"Just a moment. While you are here, let me tell you something," whispered Ali while he was struggling to remove the lid of the honey jar.

"What's up?"

"As you know, there are simultaneous protests in Tehran, Isfahan, and Tabriz universities. Saber had a meeting with the Cultural Units from other colleges in the city last night. They were talking about our strategy to join the movement."

Ali handed me a piece of paper.

"What's this?" I asked, quite surprised.

"This is sort of an announcement. An invitation for everybody to get involved and the reasons behind this movement."

Jalal added, "That's not all. The government agents arrested the head of the Cultural Unit at Tehran University last night. No one has a clue where he is now. No one is able to trace him. His family asked police and university about him, but they didn't receive an answer."

I glanced at the announcement, scanning it quickly. "This is terrible. We must do something. How can we support them? How will this protest work?"

Ali continued, "This is the first statement to inform everybody about the recent situation in other cities. We are planning a demonstration in front of the university headquarters as the next step. But first, we must raise awareness among all students. Everyone must know the current circumstances in other places. We'll stick this announcement on the Cultural Unit's board in the primary hall tomorrow and distribute it all over the university. We'll start to spread it in the dorm tonight."

"I can pass it to my friends and classmates, too."

"Yes, please. That would be helpful. The more we let people know about it, the more we can support the Tehran movement."

"As far as I'm aware, the objective is to cut the non-student governmental sources from the Basij Organization, meaning only students can be the members of the Basij Organization with no link to the regime. This means we are going to war against them. Am I right?"

Ali sipped his tea. "Yes and no. We are simply asking for legal action as per regulations. We don't want a fight. This is our fundamental right as students, and it is crystal clear in the university rules that all undergraduate organizations shall be run only by university students."

"What do you mean?"

"As part of the Science and Education Ministry's legislation, student organizations within universities must be managed and run *only* by students from that university. Non-student members or students from other colleges aren't allowed to be members. More importantly, it is stated that no private or government organization has the right to meddle in student organizations. Only university headquarters has the authority to intervene if required."

"University headquarters? What does it mean? That is a loophole, as the university authorities are from the government, and they are always controlled by the Ministry of Intelligence. Everybody knows it."

"Yes, this is the grey area! Anyway, keep in mind that the ultimate reason for the protest is demanding freedom. The freedom of the Tehran Cultural Unit leader, and subsequently, the freedom of speech."

Jalal stood up and opened the window for fresh air, but quickly shut it back as it made inside a bit cold. He turned back to me. "We are approaching the new year and not long after the end of the term. Everybody will be busy with exams and soon after will be the summer holidays. The Basij Organization is using this situation as leverage to quell the movement. The closer we get to final exams, the less support we'll have from students. So, we have to start now. Our time frame is limited."

"You are right. Time is not on our side. So, let's do it!" I said, standing up and putting a bunch of announcements in my backpack. We shook hands and I left the dormitory building.

It was late in the afternoon when I reached University Boulevard and decided to walk for a while. Walking had always helped me to sort out my thoughts like I was meditating. *Taban, Babak, financial records, the Basij Organization, the Tehran movement, protests, the announcement, the demonstration, final exams, the Science Committee magazine...* I tried to prioritise my thoughts but had no success as my mind was like an ocean and my thoughts like free fish darting everywhere.

Farid was in his room studying for upcoming exams when I arrived. "Where have you been all day? You missed two classes," he asked me, stretching his hands over his head.

"You won't believe it. I got him. I got him!"

"What the hell are you talking about?" chuckled Farid and half-rose behind his study desk.

"Babak!" I drank a glass of water without a pause. "He's sucking money from everywhere like a vacuum cleaner."

"What?" laughed Farid. "Are you alright?"

In less than five minutes I summarized the last eight hours in such a way that Farid would not get bored and then, handed him the announcement. Farid rarely involved himself in student activities, or rather, he always kept his distance from politics and other similar troubles. He glanced at the paper. "Nima, this is bloody dangerous. Do you really understand what you are up to? Be so careful, pal." He paused for some minutes and read the entire statement. After moments of silence, he added, "Anyway, this is the right thing to do."

I scratched my eyebrow. "I know. I know. I won't do anything risky. It is just to inform others about the situation in different cities."

"Nima, what about the exams? You must study more, or you'll be in deep shit. You might not pass the semester."

"I know" was my short answer that was puffed out in a short sigh.

IV

The following day, I spotted some changes on the Cultural Unit board. Glancing at the board, I passed by it fast as I was in a rush to find Taban before the first tutorial. It was early in the morning and the corridor wasn't busy. I first headed to the Science Committee room, but the door was locked. I didn't bother to open it and hastily walked upstairs to the classroom.

Abbas and Reza were talking with Farid in front of the door. Shaking hands, I gave Abbas and Reza the announcement and briefly explained it. Chatting about supporting the protest, I spotted Taban at the other end of the corridor, walking towards the classroom with her friends. I excused myself and approached her.

"Good morning, Miss Pakzad. Can I talk to you for a second?"

"Good day. Sure, what's going on?"

Her friends continued walking to the classroom, leaving us alone in the corridor.

"Can we chat in the committee room? I don't want someone overhearing us," I asked, glancing around.

"What? We have a lecture to attend now. Can't it wait till after our class?"

"It can, but I'd like to talk with you in private. This is important. No one is in the Science Committee now. After the course, everyone will be busy."

She didn't ask any more questions, but her eyebrows raised a bit and she stared right into my eyes for a few seconds.

We turned back and walked hurriedly as the tutorial was about to start. I was trying to find a proper phrase to open up the conversation, but it was more difficult than I had imagined. Entering the committee room, I closed the door and asked her to sit. Looking around without any reason, I finally sat down in front of her on the opposite side of the table.

"Can I trust you, Miss Pakzad?"

It just slipped out of my mouth. Her shiny eyes became a bit larger, and a couple wrinkles appeared on her forehead as I picked up a shadow of confusion on her face.

"Yes, of course. You are acting a bit weird!"

"Um," I cleared my throat. "How can I say this? You know that I have trusted you since the beginning of our relationship, and I trust you now, too," I murmured while vigilantly aiming to articulate the right words in my mind before shooting them out.

"I trust you, too, Mr. Zarin. What are you trying to tell me?"

"How much did you give Babak to publish the magazine?"

"What? Ten thousand. Why do you ask? I don't understand."

"Do you have any records of Science Committee financial transactions?"

She thought for some moments, then said, "I think so. Why?"

"What I'm about to tell you is super confidential. Please do not tell anyone, especially Babak."

Knowing Taban and Babak were spending time together, I managed to keep calm and pretend I did not know about their relationship. I had a strong feeling that I needed to trust her, and an even stronger desire to stick to my gut.

"What's happening, Mr. Zarin?" she asked impatiently, raising her voice a bit while staring at me, no longer hiding her concern.

I took out the expense receipt from my backpack and showed her. For the next ten minutes or so, I explained the gaps between financial records. I told her the whole story about the Science Committee magazine and how I'd found this mismatch. The more I explained what had happened, the more I got excited. "Do you see? Less than a half! The actual cost is way less than what he claimed and gathered. And this doesn't include the income from selling the journals, which he had promised to pay you back with."

Taban did not say a word. Her shimmering black eyes were pinned on the receipt. "I cannot believe it," were the pleasing words for me that finally came out of her mouth and sank inside me.

Finding more confidence in my plan, I told her what I'd discussed with Ali and Jalal the other day without naming them. "It is better if I can gather more proof and evidence. This is why I asked you if you had any bills, receipts, or records in your possession. Call it embezzlement or whatever, but I want to get to the bottom of it. This includes your money, too. It is important for me to take *your* money back. But please keep this between us for now."

"Yes, sure. I won't say anything to anyone. I think I have some records at my apartment. He told me not to keep them here at uni," she said feebly, then stood up to head out. I could see the bitter disbelief in her gaze, and that bitter look spread the weird sweetness under my skin.

I got up, too. "Thank you, Miss Pakzad."

She shook her head and left the room.

It was about nine o'clock and I had already missed half of my class, so I decided to pay a visit to the magazine publisher and make sure the delivery would be on time. An unusual feeling of satisfaction formed a smile on my face, which quickly faded away with a touch of fear. I was not sure if Taban could keep this with herself and not share it with Babak. *Taban won't tell him! How would Babak react if he found out I am behind this? He has many friends and different connections all over the college.*

The journals were ready the day after, all printed, bound, and evenly packed. "Do you want us to send it later or do you want to pick them up now?" Javad, the shop owner, asked me.

Four medium-size packages were laid on top of each other near the entrance door. "I'll take them." I called a cab and sat in the backseat. Looking at the packages, I repeated my plan and tried to convince myself that I had made the right decision. *I'll tell Babak that we are aware of what he has done. But first, I must get Borhan on my side. Now!*

Borhan was an experienced member of the committee, and had not gotten along with Babak during the last couple of years. He had entered the college one year after Babak and never had a chance to lead the Committee. Recently, we had talked at the college's café, and he had brought up his interest in taking over Babak's role when he graduated.

The cab arrived at the university and stopped just a few inches behind the central gate's boom. "Can you please let me in?" I asked the security guy, showing my student ID. The security man sat in a small cabin, staring at me without blinking. "I have a few heavy packages of journals for the Engineering College." I explained more but he did not let the cab in without the registered car permit. I tried to convince him that I couldn't drag four packages of magazines all the way to the Engineering College, but he did not care at all, just kept staring at me and slowly shaking his hairy face from inside his cage. "A rule is a rule. I cannot let you in with that car. Each car must have the permit sign."

"Oh, come on, man! What rule? I'm a student at this university and have four heavy packages in this cab. He'll drop me off and be back in a minute."

"No. The cab cannot enter."

Pulling out the magazines from the backseat, I unloaded the packages in front of the security gate and let the cab go. I went closer to the security cabin and asked him to keep his eyes on the packages until I fetched someone to help carry them in. He did not bother to utter a single word, but indolently nodded his head.

A group of girls in full black hijab were wandering near the central gate. Their black chadors were flying in the wind and made them look like a group of giant bats. The university bus from the gate had just entered the area and stopped near the Engineering College. Students were getting out of the bus and hanging around the café and parking lots for a while. It was almost the end of the lunchtime and students were everywhere. Keeping my eyes on the magazines from a distance and walking around the crowd, I arrived at the college and darted into the Science Committee room.

Borhan was talking with two committee members about new software tutorials. I jumped in and said, "Sorry to interrupt you, but I brought the magazines. They are ready! I left them at the central gate's security. Can you take care of them? I need to head to my class now."

Borhan smiled. "Excellent. This is very good news. Thanks a lot. You go to your course, and we'll carry them right now!"

I glanced at Borhan and whispered, "Um… I need to talk to you for a moment. Let's talk while we go to the class."

He seemed a bit puzzled and asked the other boys to put the journals in the room's cabinet and lock it till he came back.

I patted Borhan's shoulder and asked him to follow me. "Let's walk. I have to tell you something, but no one must find out about it."

He stopped and stared at me with a half-open mouth. "What?" He muttered as his eyes behind the thick glasses zoomed on me, waiting for an explanation.

"Let's walk, buddy. Come on."

He could not resist anymore and without hiding his curiosity, asked, "What's happening, Nima? Is everything alright? Don't you have a class to attend?"

"Don't worry. I'll explain it. But first, let's get out of here."

Walking near the amphitheatre, we headed to the Faculty of Science. We went inside the building and moved to a cosy café which was located underground. I bought two cups of tea, and we sat down at a small table at the end of the room. Borhan was shaking his legs nonstop and looking around.

"Borhan, what I'm about to tell you has to stay between us. You are the only person I can trust and I'm sure you can manage it very well." I tried not to be so patronizing. Then I started to tell him the details about Babak and how he was taking advantage of the system. I showed him the receipt for the magazines and told him I had more evidence. My words flew to his ears neatly in an exact order that I practiced.

His legs stopped shaking, but instead, he touched his chin with his right hand, tightly held the receipt with his left hand, and slowly moved around in his chair. "This is embezzlement!"

"Whatever you want to call it. It doesn't matter. The point is that we sort out this issue professionally and fast."

"Sort it out? How?"

"I have a plan." I sipped my tea, leaned a bit towards him, and whispered my words out like a top-secret mission. "Borhan, listen. I'll talk to Babak and tell him that we are aware of everything. We, meaning you and I. Then I'll tell him to hand over the committee money and step down with an excuse about his graduation. You'll then take over and lead the Science Committee."

Borhan left the receipt at the table, leaned back and stretched his legs with folded arms. "What if he denies it, or doesn't agree to resign?" he asked with a different tone, like he was getting ready for plan B and even C.

"Don't worry about it. He doesn't have any other choice. I know how to convince him. But keep in mind that this is important to not tell anyone else. We must take care of this mess quietly. Are you with me?"

Borhan stared at me without saying a word.

"Are you with me?" I asked again.

He leaned forward in his chair, unfolded his arms, and eyed around. "Yes, yes. I won't tell anybody."

"Good on you. Once Babak steps down, I'll ask for an internal poll and convince everybody to vote for you."

"Sounds like a plan."

V

Deep down, I knew it was not all about correcting the system, but mainly about my feelings for Taban. I was getting more and more obsessed with finding additional evidence against Babak as we started to sell the magazines at the university the week after. It was not an easy task, and I spent a considerable amount of time managing the distribution of journals between several colleges while I kept my eyes on the income. At the same time, Taban brought me the additional receipts and some other notes from the committee's finance logbook. Reviewing them line by line, I spotted some further mismatches, as I had expected. Although they were not significant, but it was enough to give me full confidence about my decision to take out Babak in my own way.

It was a quiet Monday with continuous wind that kept the entire sky clear of clouds. A group of students, all in winter jackets, was standing near the entrance. I overheard them talking about demonstration and protest as I entered the building, where a quiet day suddenly turned into one resonating with howling, unrecognizable voices. I craned my neck and looked around while stepping forward cautiously. A crowd of students, mostly boys, were in the salon adjacent to the Cultural Unit board, arguing about something loudly. Saber, Jalal, and other members of the Cultural Unit were standing in front of the Unit's board like a human shield. Faces from the Basij Organization were gathered around in front of the human shield. Amin was at the other end of the salon, waving his hand towards me. I hardly manoeuvred my way through the crowd and approached him.

"What's happening?" I asked quietly.

"The Basij Organization lost their temper again. They are insisting on taking the new announcement down from the Cultural Unit board. Saber has been arguing with them for about half an hour. This could get nasty."

Voices echoed inside the salon, and it was difficult to understand who was saying what. Saber was talking loudly to the audiences around the board, but I couldn't hear him, so I moved to the other side of the salon. His forehead was like an accordion, full of wrinkles, and his neck muscles were getting tense to the extent that I was afraid a vein might explode.

"This is to support our fellow students in other cities. We are demanding clarity, justice, and equality!" shouted Saber firmly.

I had never seen Saber raise his voice and talk with anger, but at that very moment, he was a different person. I noticed the Basij members were beginning to leave the area gradually, trying not to draw any further attention. Not long after, Saber finished his speech and stormed to the Cultural Unit, so did I.

"What was that all about?" I asked Saber as we entered the Cultural Unit room.

"Those fanatics wanted to break our board and take the announcement down! I had expected that reaction when I hung the new announcement there late night." He was almost out of breath. Amin directed him to sit down near the window to calm down for a moment.

Jalal said, "They claimed the statement in our board was against the university and Islamic rules. Bullshit! Whatever they don't like is automatically categorized as acting against Islam!"

I looked at Jalal. "So, what's going to happen next?"

Saber replied in anger, "No idea. Most probably they've already reported to the Ministry of Intelligence. The announcement is linked to Tehran's protest. Do you remember the missing student from Tehran University? It turned out the government agents took him for interrogation. He was released this morning, but the university expelled him for acting against Islamic regulations."

Jalal and Amin tried to calm Saber. I gave him a glass of water and didn't ask anything more as my mind flew somewhere else.

I left them after a few minutes and headed to the Science Committee to find Babak. It was getting quieter in the corridor. Babak was in the committee room, chatting with his friends about his final thesis.

"Have you seen what just happened outside?" I asked them.

"Yes, this is just the beginning. The Cultural Unit team impressively stood up against them. That was a brave move," answered Babak proudly like that was his speech.

"Yes, it was indeed the right thing to do." I paused. "Do you have a minute? We need to talk."

Babak glanced at his friends and said, "Yes, is everything okay?"

"Yes, let's have a walk."

"As you wish." Babak shrugged.

I brought him to the same café in the Faculty of Science. It was not so busy, and we found a quiet spot. I asked if he wanted tea or anything else, and he declined. I bought two cups of tea anyway and sat in front of him on the other side of the table.

"So, what's so important that you brought me here?"

"Borhan reached out to me last night." I had been practicing this scenario for a few days.

"Borhan?" he chuckled. "What for?"

"How can I say this? Listen, pal. There is no easy way to bring it up. He presented rock-solid evidence that you took money from the committee budget."

Babak turned pale and his smile vanished.

"What the fuck?" he shouted furiously.

"Listen to me. Borhan explained the gap between actual expenses and the amount of money you claim. I told him it had to be a misunderstanding. There must be a reason behind it, but he was not convinced. Borhan was talking about the sugar factory tour and showed me the bills for training courses. The last one was the magazine expenditure. None of the real payments matched the expenses you reported to the university finance department."

Babak was listening without moving a single muscle. I paused, leaned back, and stared at his face. His tightened lips and pulled down eyebrows were not enough for me.

I wasn't sure if he bought what I'd just said, so I continued, "Babak, you are my friend. I don't know what is happening, but Borhan gathered a bunch of goddamn evidence—you name it, bills, receipts! He was about to report this as an embezzlement case to the university's Human Resources Department, but I told him to hold on for now."

Babak started moving his legs under the table, and continuously tapped on the table with his fingers.

I asked, "Babak, I need to know the truth. You can trust me."

Babak slowly shook his head to left and right a couple of times, stopped tapping, and then spoke. "It's all bullshit!"

"Okay, okay. Calm down." I became a bit nervous but didn't back off. "I asked Borhan to hold off on reporting this mess till I could talk with you. I told him that there should be another way to resolve this issue."

"What way?" His eyes narrowed behind his glasses.

That was the moment I had been waiting for. I gained more confidence after hearing that question.

"Well, you can hand over the money and step down. I've already convinced Borhan that the right thing to do is *not* to report you to HR. You are in your last semester and leaving uni in a few months. You can resign with the excuse that you need to finish your thesis and give the cash to Borhan. No one needs to know anything else."

Babak seemed tense and edgy, but managed to ask prudently, "Who else knows about it?"

"Miss Pakzad."

VI

Babak called a meeting the next day and handed in his resignation. He gave some money to Borhan a few days later, not the total amount, but we didn't push him for more. The Science Committee members nominated Borhan and voted for him to lead the unit. It was crystal clear to me that Babak and Taban had not talked again; it was so comforting like a warm afternoon's siesta at a golden sand beachside.

The cold, dry winter was in its last few weeks. It was early evening, and the soft, glowing twilight made the horizon stunningly picturesque. I was the only person in the Science Committee room, sitting behind the computer desk near the window and looking out to the college backyard. Rubbing my fingers together, I thought about the upcoming months, final exams, finishing the second semester, and wrapping up my first year. Although the door was fully open, I couldn't hear anything in the hallway. Almost no one was in the building as all classes had finished for the day. I had a plan to review the last mathematics sessions with Farid, Abbas, and Reza in the dormitory after dinner, so I turned off the computer, pushed the chair slightly backward and got ready to leave the room.

Slightly bending to find my backpack under the computer desk, I heard someone call my name.

"Hi, Nima. I was hoping to find you here."

I jumped a bit as I had not expected anyone. There was Taban standing in front of the door.

"Oh, sorry, I didn't mean to scare you." She chuckled tenderly.

I laughed, too. "Miss Pakzad. Yes, you scared the hell out of me, but I'm very happy to see you. What are you doing here?" I noticed that she had not called me by my surname. It was the very first time she called me Nima, and not Mr. Zarin.

She stepped in and left the door open. Her eyes seemed brighter. A bunch of black hair hung out of her khimar down to her chin like a silky waterfall. Glancing around the room, she opened her handbag and took out a small, rectangular box, beautifully wrapped with silver and gold gift paper. A purple flower made from shiny ribbon was attached to the box. Gripping it with her fingers, she stretched her hand towards me and whispered, "This is a small gift for you. Just to say thanks for everything."

My heart was beating fast and every cell in my body was getting warmer and warmer. Looking at her red nails, I quivered from inside and eagerly took the gift. "Thanks a lot, Miss Pakzad. I'm speechless. Um… Very kind of you, um… But why?"

She stared at me. Her gaze penetrated my brain, making me numb, and unable to put words together suitably. She leaned a bit to the left, glanced at her hands, and turned her eyes back to me. "I once trusted a man who did not deserve it. I found myself in a relationship that gave me nothing but cynicism. And then, you showed up."

I had no idea what to say, or how to react. My feet could not feel the ground. I was absolutely powerless while I tried to process the meaning of what she had just told me. Goosebumps spread along my arms. "Thank you" were the only words muttered out. I gently unwrapped the gift box and tried to avoid looking at her eyes. It was a golden-capped pen with a silver body. What a sensational moment. I felt elated like I had never felt that way. It was like a world of blessing opened its door, inviting me to embrace eternal happiness. It was one of those first moments in life that was unlikely to happen again. "This is magnificent. Thank you so much, Miss Pakzad."

"Thank *you*, Nima. And please, call me Taban."

"Taban, sure."

"Very well, I'm gonna go now. Have a good evening."

"Um, Taban," I whispered.

"Yes?"

"Um, would you like to go to a café, or a restaurant sometime? Um, I mean, together?" I could not breathe properly, and my chest moved up and down fast, but I managed to finish my sentence.

"I'd love to! Anytime."

CHAPTER 6

I

The first academic year had gone by so fast with all its ups and downs. Most of the students travelled back to their hometown during the summer holiday, but I decided to stay and take two courses which I had failed last year. It was the only way to close the gap between myself and my classmates, in particular, Taban. I told my parents about the failing courses as they kept asking me to take a break and visit them during the summer, but I didn't say a word about my blossoming friendship with Taban. I didn't know why but it wasn't because I wanted to hide it from them. It was too much for me to open up, talk about my true feelings for Taban, bring up my covert emotions and picture my dreams.

The university was totally different in the summer. The parking lot was deserted and there was no gathering in the backyard, which meant no smoke, no laughter, and no chitchat. Just a few students popped up in the café during those days, and I had no mood to stay there alone longer than it took me to eat something fast and easy like a sausage sandwich or a cup of tea. The corridor was so quiet in comparison to normal school days. Walking along the passageway, I barely saw any open doors; almost all the units took time off during the summer.

Outside, the blazing sun wasn't showing any sign of mercy until a bit before dusk, when a comforting zephyr descended to Earth, weaving through the thousands of plain trees over the city, and softly blowing the languorous heatwave away. Usually, I wandered around Azad Park after my classes, or in the early evening as many people hung around there. I liked strolling in crowded places, unleashing my desires, and picturing my dreams. I often thought about Taban and how I could take our flourishing relationship to the next level—and by next level, I meant the first level.

It was extremely difficult for me to reveal my genuine sentiments and show Taban my true emotions. Tonnes of thoughts pushed me away and held me back whenever I was about to show her my real feelings. Overthinking the embarrassment of being rejected, combined with society's cultural and religious beliefs had smashed my confidence every time I stared into her eyes and felt the craving to caress her silky hair, and rest my lips on hers.

It was during those sizzling days when I often tried to picture my future in the next ten years or more, not to plan anything, but to release my wishes and let them fly wherever they desired. It wasn't as easy as it sounded. I was somehow incapable of comprehending a glamorous future and visualizing eternal happiness. It was like imagining a colour that I'd never seen in my life or looking for something that I didn't have a clue about it. Maybe that summer brought up for me the darkness of real life, and I had been destined to grasp the deeper meaning of the incomprehensible human existence. The absurdity of day-to-day life was magnified—life seemed to be a cycle of being born, growing up, learning some things, and then repeatedly doing some other things till finally turning to dust, while pathetically hoping for redemption. Whatever it was, I detested the agonizing loneliness during those long, quiet days.

I tried not to stay in my underground apartment too much. Farid had gone back to Tehran as soon as the second semester finished, and I was on my own. Visiting my relatives or catching up with Amin were helpful in lifting my spirit during the blazing summer. My parents also visited me for a week, which was an absolute emotional boost. The university was unbearable without Taban. Frustrated by the repetitive tutorials in empty classes, I decided to spend more time on one of my ideas about the functionality of religions. The research was not new activity for me but soon led me to an ideological turning point. I had been reading, talking with diverse individuals, and gathering people's interpretations of religions during the academic year. I had had enough time to put everything together and categorize others' opinions. Interviewing more than fifty people, I had collected something like a tiny human-beliefs database, each of them, in some way, had a unique definition of God, and insight into religions. They ranged from an extremist fanatic woman who had been brainwashed her entire life to an open-minded middle-aged guy who didn't believe in God at all. I had more than enough time to review all the interviews in detail; and I did that.

It was that summer when I experienced a deep crack in my fundamental beliefs, which later ended up being a total denial of that deceptive illusion— the almighty concept called God in all religions.

II

On one of those long, hot sunny days, I had just finished my morning classes and was about to go for an early lunch when I noted Amin standing near the college primary entrance. His white polo shirt with a popped collar made his sun-tanned face look a bit darker.

"Are you going to the canteen?" he asked me out of the blue.

"Yes. What are you doing here?"

"I was waiting for you, buddy. Let's go to my place and have lunch there."

"What?" I chuckled.

"Ali wants to talk with you. Come on, pal. Let's go. I'm starving." He patted my back, and his muscular biceps caught my eyes.

"Ali? When did he come back? He wants to talk with me? What about?"

"Oh, don't be silly. He wants to chat with you over the phone. Do you have a landline? No! So, let's go."

"Any idea what it is about?" I asked Amin on our way.

"Something about the protest and his plan for the new academic year. Saber and Ali had a few meetings in Tehran this summer. Um, not sure what they are exactly up to."

He led me to his beige Nissan Armada and we hopped in. As he drove, he asked me about my summer courses with frequent pauses between every other word, not stammering, but as was his style. The streets were not too busy, and we arrived at his house by noon.

The first thing that Amin did was to turn on the AC. "Oh man, swimming would be nice now." He sighed, then added that his parents had gone to Turkey for summer vacation, but he had to stay to run their pistachio farm. "They should be by the beach now. Oh, boy! Let's eat something."

I was curious to find out what was happening with Ali and Saber. "Forget about lunch, buddy. Call Ali please."

"As you wish." Amin gave me the phone receiver. "Just redial the last incoming number," then he walked to the kitchen.

"Hello? Ali? It's Nima."

It was pleasant to talk with Ali over the phone as we hadn't been in touch since he left for the summer holiday. It turned out that Ali and Saber had frequently visited the government opposition front-liners during the last few weeks. Ali didn't explain everything in detail over the phone, but he asked me to book the university amphitheatre and coordinate a gathering for the next term. "Mr. Mohseni has agreed to come over in autumn and present a brand-new seminar for all students. We can obtain the permit under Cultural Unit's name. Um… The seminar title could be something like the Culture of Democracy!"

I knew a little about Mr. Mohseni. Ali and Saber sometimes talked about him when we gathered together. He'd been part of the Islamic regime for years, but had gradually separated from the body of the power and turned out to be sort of an opposition leader. He had resigned from his government posts and founded a cultural journalism NGO. Since then, he'd actively criticized the governing systems and become a voice of oppositions inside the country. Having him at the university would be a massive support to the student movement and could give a boost to the protest.

"So, what should I do?" I asked Ali with unhidden excitement.

"For now, we should set an exact date, send a request to reserve the amphitheatre, and begin advertising for this seminar."

"What about permit?"

"Don't worry. Saber is on it."

We discussed Mr. Mohseni's seminar preparation for a few more minutes, and then I hung up the phone, just in time for the lunch as Amin came out of the kitchen with two plates in his hands.

"Smell's mouth-watering!" I said, and we had our lunch in front of the TV.

The blistering summer was finally coming to an end. I successfully passed my exams and sorted out the preliminary preparations for Mr. Mohseni's seminar. I booked the university amphitheatre for mid-October and printed out two hundred flyers. The plan was to distribute them in the first week of the new academic year. I had two more weeks to go before the new semester, so I bought a train ticket and departed to Tehran, my hometown. I had to change my mood and find relief for the invisible pressure. I had not realized I missed my friends and family so much till I paid them a visit. The short trip back home helped me lift my spirits and get ready to start my second year at university: the year my life changed forever.

CHAPTER 7

(Second Year)

I

Sitting in the college's café, I eyed around while waiting for the first course of the year. The familiar faces, a messy queue in front of the cashier, sudden laughter from other tables, vague voices from the girls' section, clanking noises of metallic trays and plates, and the pungent smell of fried onions with sausage from the kitchen all reminded me that I was not a beginner anymore, and it felt great.

Sitting in front of me were Ali, Amin, and Jalal with takeaway cups of tea in their hands, while Farid and Saber sat near me on the other side of the table having their breakfast. Ali had a new haircut, a bit shorter than usual and Saber had lost a couple of kilograms over the summer holiday. Students were waving and shaking hands as soon as they saw each other. Farid was checking out new students while talking with Amin and talked about his new hobby, tennis. He had bought a tennis racket and passed a couple of training sessions during the summer. Amin was a skilled tennis player, so they were setting up a plan to practise together during the year while Ali and Saber were discussing student protests in other cities. They'd had several meetings with other activists from different universities during the last two and a half months of summer vacation. Loud music from the café speakers and the rumbling of students near the café entrance were frequently interrupting our chat. Ali briefly explained Mr. Mohseni's seminar and his agenda, then he talked about an integrated anti-government demonstration in all universities, which had started the year before.

I couldn't focus on the topic as my mind was somewhere else. A haystack of feathery excitement was mounting inside me as I was counting down to see Taban soon. For the entire summer, I had been looking forward to meeting her again, but I had yet to see her since she left for the holidays. It was almost time to attend the first course of the year and it meant it was about the time to meet Taban. We cleaned up the mess on our table and threw the paper cups in a bin near the entrance.

Saber turned to me. "The technical subjects are getting more serious this semester. You have two difficult courses, and these aren't the tutorials you want to mess with."

Farid overheard him and leaned towards us. "Heat and Material Balance is one of them. Abbas told me the professor isn't willing to pass anyone."

Saber chuckled. "Thermodynamics is the fundamental course for mechanical engineering and needs extra effort."

I nodded my head and smiled. "There is nothing to be worried about. This term is going to be fine unless I screw it up again!"

As much as I was excited to see Taban, I did not want to express my eagerness to others. However, Farid picked it up and whispered in my ear, "Don't worry, buddy. You'll meet her soon." He winked.

"Shut up." I grinned, opened the classroom's door, and looked for Taban like she was the only reason I entered the room. I found her on the spot, standing near the professor's podium with other girls. Taban turned back the moment she heard the creaking door open like she was waiting for me, too, as her twinkling eyes flashed. It seemed that she had felt my presence at that moment.

Farid glanced at me and gently poked my hip.

The girls stopped chatting for a moment and glanced at us. Farid nodded his head at them, then changed his direction to the end of the classroom, where Abbas and Reza were grinning at us and waving their hands.

Taban stared at me with her thick red lips and glowing smile. She wore a short outer garment, a black khimar, dark blue jeans, and shiny Chelsea boots.

I waved at Abbas and Reza while an ecstatic force pushed me towards Taban.

"Glad to see you, Mr. Zarin. I'm very happy you passed your summer courses so we can be in the same classes again," Taban said, and the other girls followed her lead by asking about the summer courses and the college during the holidays. For a few seconds, I sank inside an illusional lake of emotions as I wished if everyone could just disappear for a few minutes so I could be alone with Taban at that moment. The words that came out of my mouth weren't the same as the ones I'd practiced saying to Taban upon seeing her again. The girls continued by chatting about the new semester's subjects till the professor walked in.

"There we go, ladies. The second year is officially started. Good luck to all of us," I said quickly, and took my seat near Farid. Taban smiled and sat in her usual spot, staring at me.

II

In less than a week, Saber had managed to sort out the permit for Mr. Mohseni's seminar, and right after that, we began distributing the invitation flyers all over the university.

"How did you get the permit? I didn't expect the Islamic Council would approve it!" I asked Saber over lunch.

"It wasn't me. Mr. Mohseni has some connections in the system. They sorted it out," murmured Saber and winked at me.

The seminar was in a week and the Cultural Unit's team was extremely busy with all the preparation. Ali and Jalal were worried about the security of the gathering. I never saw them like that before—being extra vigilant with a touch of paranoia. Rumour had it that the Basij Organization would not let Mr. Mohseni carry out his speech without trouble.

"You don't need to worry," Mr. Mohseni told us the night before his seminar. "I've seen these sorts of things a lot in the past. What are they going to do? Throw bottles at me? Swear? Disrupt my speech?" He smirked. I wasn't sure if he was sarcastic or not, till he cleared the air for me. "The more they make a mess, the better everybody sees their real faces. I got used to it, and you'll get used to it, too."

I had accompanied Ali, Saber, and Jalal to visit Mr. Mohseni in his hotel after his arrival. He was in his fifties, grey hair, and a clean-shaven face. He had a trivial sense of humour and spoke with a soft tone, clear, and intentional with his words. He described to us the recent governmental roadmap in order to manage the academic system and how it was ultimately impacting the students. He explained more about the variety of tasks within his cultural journalism NGO and the extensive support from students in different cities. Saber and Ali asked some questions about the students' protest and new movement against the suppressive system, while I was all ears.

It was the first time in my life I'd been able to sit near a famous politician—or rather, influential government opposition. Listening to his ideas and plans, I visualized a feeble, shivering light at the end of the dark, suffocating tunnel.

The seminar began at about six o'clock without delay. The amphitheatre was packed with students who had come from all colleges in the city. "That's awesome! All seats are taken.

We've got a full house!" I said quite excitedly to Anna and Taban, and then headed behind the scenes. Unrecognizable voices from the students tangled together and filled the entire salon with a uniform humming sound. Most of the seats were filled with boys, however, a fairly sizeable group of girls found their spots in a separate section designated for ladies. Taban and Anna were helping the Cultural Unit to take care of the girls' section while I was behind the scenes double-checking the cassette tape that I'd prepared for the seminar.

The first track was the national anthem. Playing the tape upon Saber's signal, the crowd rose from their seats and the entire amphitheatre went silent. A few minutes later, Saber walked onto the stage and briefly introduced Mr. Mohseni by listing his years of services to the country. Then he glanced at me. I had selected a famous revolutionary song for that moment. Looking back at Saber, I pushed the play button on the tape player and the gigantic speakers around the salon turned into thundering boxes.

"Our homeland has fallen in darkness,
It's a sin to sit in this darkness and do nothing,
Give back my gun, I must defend my homeland,
Give back my gun, I must get my freedom back..."

Listening to that stimulating song, I murmured it word by word as if all my cells craved to shout them. The song echoed in the amphitheatre, energized the air and soon the crowd started repeating it. I got goosebumps from the wave of the audience's applause at the end of the song.

A moment later, Mr. Mohseni headed to the stage and stood behind the wooden podium. I was standing a couple of meters away, eager to figure out what he had to say as he glanced at me, smiled, and turned back to the crowd. "That was a sensational song, and it brought back lots of memories from those old days." He paused for a moment. "But we don't talk with guns in our hands, anymore. We passed that era a long time ago. It is now time to learn how to resolve our differences with *talking*."

The whole salon exploded into clapping and whistling. Clapping aside the other students, I felt a bit embarrassed. *I should've selected another song! He didn't like it*, I thought.

Mr. Mohseni continued by introducing his NGO, explaining the organization's mission, and describing associated activities within the bureau. It wasn't long before he brought up the student protests around the country, explained the key reasons behind them, touched on their demands, and linked it to individuals' fundamental rights within each society. A slight humming sound came out of the crowd as people began speaking. I looked around to find out the source, but could not spot it.

Mr. Mohseni took a sip of water and continued, "History shows us that absolute power of any sort eventually leads to corruption and gradually degrades society. The worst type is, indeed, an ideological autocracy."

Suddenly, a small group of audience stood up and shouted, "Israel's spy! Israel's spy!" They were about eighteen to twenty men wearing brown military pants and plain black shirts. They started moving towards the stage and kept shouting, "Death to Israel! Death to Israel!"

Some of the students in the amphitheatre began to boo those men, and just in a couple of seconds, almost the entire audience chanted against the men in brown military pants, "Get out! Get out!" Saber and Jalal were trying to reach the men and move them out of the amphitheatre. Some students rose from the front row and blocked the way to the stage protecting Mr. Mohseni from the men in brown military pants while those men started to push the other students, provoking the crowd to get physical.

Ali ran onto the stage and led Mr. Mohseni out of the amphitheatre through the backstage door. Saber yelled at other students in the front row, "Calm down! Don't fight! Calm down!" Half of the unknown men slowly left the salon through the front emergency door, and the other half was still shouting in the salon. Saber raced onto the stage, took the microphone, and repeatedly asked everybody to calm down and leave the salon without fighting. It didn't take more than ten minutes for the other half of those men to storm out of the doorways and disappear into the crowd.

After wrapping everything up, Saber and Jalal took a cab to Mr. Mohseni's hotel to check on him. Farid, Taban, and I decided to walk back to our apartments after the crowd was almost gone and the amphitheatre settled down. On our way back, along University Boulevard, Farid glanced at me and Taban, puffed out a thin cloud of steamy breath, and said, "If you live in Iran, you cannot escape from politics. It is impossible to separate yourself from it. It surrounds everything like convoluted, toxic layers of an invisible, deceptive cloud. The farther you get into it, the more you inhale it. You feel dizzy and try to understand what the hell is going on around you, unaware of the rapid rising of the fatal dose in your blood. It is beyond your capacity, far beyond, and you can't understand. It will sooner or later cause your brain to stop functioning. This is when you reach the inevitable breaking point and turn into another person forever. You never realize when and how you will be poisoned, but it is always too late."

III

Two months passed faster than I'd expected. I had been getting closer to Taban day after day. We had decided to be more active in the Cultural Unit, rather than the Science Committee. The new election for the committee was on its way and neither I nor Taban nominated ourselves. We spent most of our time with Ali, Jalal, and Saber. The Cultural Unit had a weekly session called Book Review, which was run by Karim, who had a deep knowledge of literature on top of his charismatic character.

It was early January when Karim asked Taban and I to become members of the Book Review Club. Each week, one person presented a book to the audience, and then all students shared their different points of view. We liked the idea and joined the group. The book review sessions were always held in the early evening when classes were done for the day. Taban and I usually strolled back to our apartments together after the book review sessions. That was the best part of my week when I could spend more alone time with her, walking and talking about our dreams and wishes.

One of those happy days, I sat in the Cultural Unit room talking with Karim and Taban about the influence of existentialism on modern literature while Karim suddenly asked, "Why don't you pick a book and talk about it?"

Taban's mouth rounded for a split second, "Oh!" She winked at Karim, and then stared at me, "That sounds great. Doesn't it, Mr. Zarin?"

I chuckled, enlarged my eyes and slightly brought back my head. "This seems like an ambush!" I didn't overthink it and agreed instantly.

"So, when do you reckon you can pull it off?" Taban asked, grinning.

"Um, I'd like to present something different. Let me think about it, and then we'll talk about it at the end of the next session."

Karim stood up, stretched his hand towards me, and said, "Deal, buddy! Looking forward to it! See you this evening."

It was a cloudy day, but not so cold as to make your nose run. The sky had bizarre shades of purple reflections diffusing inside the dark clouds. That scene reminded me of *The Brothers Lionheart* story while they fight with a fire-breathing dragon to overcome tyranny. That mysterious, sorrowful theme had been engraved in my mind since childhood. However, the book session that evening had a different essence. Anna was presenting *The Alchemist* by Paulo Coelho. Brown high-heeled shoes raised her at least a couple of inches above other girls. Karim, Taban, and I were sitting near each other listening to her presentation.

"I'd love to live with that ideology—listening to my heart and following my dreams. But it's so unreal and doesn't work for me. It is like a fairy tale for adults," I whispered to Karim's ear, referring to the key character in the book.

"I think this is all about living what you believe. It may not be real for you, but it's probably true life for others," he answered confidently while Anna began to wrap up her presentation with a short Q&A. She joined us a bit later, smiled, and sat near us to rest her legs.

"That was excellent. The session went well. Good discussions at the end." Karim thanked her, then looked at me and asked, "So? Tell me something interesting."

Anna glanced at me and raised her eyebrow, curious about what Karim meant.

"Nima is willing to present something in the next event," Taban told her cheerfully.

I answered, "I'm thinking about something more than a book, and certainly need a couple of weeks to prepare it."

Karim stared at the girls and said, "He just can't stick to the plan, can he?"

I chuckled. "I'm going to open up an ideology, not just a specific book. I'd like to describe Kafka and his world and thoughts."

A bit confused, they were pleased with the suggestion.

After a moment of pause, Karim yelled, "This is a fantastic idea! A huge deal."

Knowing exactly what I wanted to deliver, I turned my face to Karim. "This might need a bit more advertisement and I believe more than an hour for the session itself. So, maybe we can sell it as a special event?"

Karim supported the proposal. "Go for it, buddy. Just give me a date."

Setting a time for the next two weeks, we all left the room together. Karim and Anna headed to their dorms and Taban and I exited the building from the main gate and walked along University Boulevard. It was a bit hazy outside, but a cold, dry wind was blowing.

"Nima, do you have enough time for everything? This semester is more difficult. I'm worried about you," Taban said while she was struggling to keep her scarf tight in the wind.

"Um, I'm not gonna lie to you. I'm not sure. Hopefully, I pass the exams. I'm trying," I answered, quietly looking around. We were cautious, or rather, we were sort of nervous about drawing police attention. After what had happened to Farid and Asal last year, we did not want the same drama at all. On one hand, it was the most satisfying feeling to wander with Taban and share our moments, but on the other hand, it was awfully stressful to walk together because of the governmental Islamic rules. I was craving to hold her hand while walking, but the fear of getting arrested always held me back. If the police or Islamic militia saw us walking shoulder to shoulder, they would ask for ID to see if we were married or not. We didn't want to be arrested or harassed. That was why I always had some hidden anxiety in the back of my mind when we were walking alone together.

IV

It was a week before my book session when Karim put up the announcement on the Cultural Unit's board, and we distributed invitations within the university.

"Religions get lost as people do."
Welcome to Franz Kafka's world.
Metamorphosis / The Castle / Amerika / The Trial

The quote from Kafka got more attention than I had anticipated. It was the first time someone had clearly posted a controversial text against religions on the official board. It didn't take long before the Basij Organization leader asked Saber to take it down. Saber said there was nothing against any religion or university law in the invitation. He also added that if they insisted on taking it away, they needed a formal order from the university headquarters as the Cultural Unit was an independent student organization and would not take orders from the Basij.

We carried out the seminar before the Basij members could do anything about it. On the day of the presentation, we were worried about their interference, but Ali told me they wouldn't create any problems. It was easy for the Basij Organization to ask Islamic militia from outside the university to raid any gathering which, in their word, was against Islamic values and turn the event into a fight zone. This was what had happened during Mr. Mohseni's seminar, and I was anxious about the same thing in my session.

As students kept entering the conference room, alone or in small groups, Karim said, "Wow, this is the first time the room has been full!"

I scanned the attendees to see any unfamiliar faces. I spotted a group of four men, sitting in the second row, talking together. I asked Karim if he knew them.

"They are from the literature faculty," he said. "They are my guests. Don't worry."

I also spotted a couple Basij members who took seats in the middle row.

I began the seminar by greeting the audience while Taban and Saber stood at the end of the class, and Anna sat in the centre, the same row as the two Basij members. Karim was standing near the entrance, and Ali and Jalal were outside in the foyer. This was the setup we'd agreed on in order to monitor the crowd and control the meeting.

I tried to keep eye contact with everybody and then started the first part of my seminar. "You can't find an effect without a real cause. This is a fact. And there is always at least one reason behind reading any book! Sometimes you want to understand a new ideology; other times you are willing to learn a new skill; under certain circumstances you might want to know more about Salvador Dalí; one time in life you have to pass the thermodynamics exam; and most of the time, we like the cover design! So, there is always a reason to read!"

The crowd cheered up with some quiet, short laughter and I got the feedback I was looking for. After a brief pause, I continued. "I'd just finished *The Queen's Necklace* by Alexandre Dumas. I was about sixteen years old and totally in love with Dumas's masterpieces. The way he explained the historical events in France and the details of the revolution, combined with a series of romantic stories and missionary movements astonished me at that time. Anyway, it was about two o'clock, and I couldn't sleep. I was lost in my thoughts, a bit upset, and kept asking myself about what book to read next, what book to read next. All of a sudden, something fell down. *Bang*! It scared me. Jumping out of my bed, I rubbed my eyes and gazed down. Believe it or not, I saw a book on the floor. It had fallen from my bookshelf and was lying down with its cover face up. I bent a bit to see the title. *The Metamorphosis*!" I stopped for a second, scanned the audiences' faces, glanced at Taban, and sipped my water. "I took the book, but did not like the cover at all as it was a drawing of a gigantic black bug on a plain, faded blue background. It was a horrible picture, particularly for the ones who just finished an incredibly colourful novel full of hidden romantic affairs! Nevertheless, I began to read it. Line by line, page by page, for the entire night. It was a clear day outside when I reached the last paragraph of the book. I couldn't bring my jaw back to the first position. I could see a massive exclamation mark on top of my head. I had been waiting the whole night to see what would happen after Gregor woke up from his nightmare. But he never did. I was so confused! The book was finished, and Gregor had never woken up. It was not a tormented dream; it was his real life!"

I finished the first part of my lecture and asked the audience to keep their questions till the end of the session. "Today, I'd like to talk about Kafka's ideology, not his publications. I'm eager to dig more on the cause rather than the effect. What was in Kafka's mind which led him to all these masterpieces?" I took three books with both hands and raised them so everyone could see as I discussed the fundamental theme within Kafka's books and explained his point of view about life, particularly religions. From time to time, I glanced at Taban, and she responded back with a smile. Expanding more on the topic of religion, I glimpsed at the two guys from the Basij Organization, raised my voice and said, "Does God exist?" I paused for a moment, then added, "That was the question in Kafka's mind." I turned to the others. "Do you believe in God? No need to answer now as you are not allowed to say anything but 'Yes' if you live in this country. Just think about it again in your very private time. Think!" I could hear the audience breathing, but not a single word. An unusual silence was all over the conference room. Touching on that forbidden subject, I pulled the trigger. "Religion is nothing but a slow-release narcotic pill for the malfunctioning brains!"

The seminar finished, and I had managed to unleash my plan.

"How was it?" I asked Taban.

"That was weirdly awesome! I loved it. So different to other seminars. Everybody liked it." She lightly clapped for me. "I have to go to the dorm to study for the upcoming exams. See you later." She winked at me and left the classroom with the other girls.

Karim congratulated me and said, "It was an interesting seminar. We've never had this much attention in the room."

"Thank you. I'm very glad."

It was getting late, and Farid was waiting for me near the door. "Are you coming with us? Amin has a car tonight!"

"Let's go, pal!"

V

Less than a week after the seminar, I was called upon by the Islamic Council. The official summons was sent to the Cultural Unit.

"Don't worry. You've been there before," said Saber, trying to change my mood.

"This isn't fair. It is insane." The words shivered out, vibrating by anger and frustration, rather than fear.

"You need to keep calm and act mature. Do you understand me?" Saber repeated as he picked up a rare rage in my voice.

"Tyrants. I hate them," I responded without looking at Saber.

"Chill out, buddy. Do you want to see your graduation or not? Being brave and doing the right thing is not always equal to fighting back and saying what is in your mind. Most of the times, you need to compromise, otherwise you can't proceed. This shit is real, and you must act prudently." Saber gazed at me and paused like he was scanning something inside his head. "You have two options: one, walk there and relieve yourself by telling them your genuine opinions about God, religion, dictatorship, democracy, and so on. Or two, walk there and bullshit them." He patted my back. "Go with the first option and in the best-case scenario, they'll expel you from the university and ban you from education forever if they don't execute you for talking against Islam and God! Take the second option and piss them off without admitting anything. This is how you should keep yourself safe and survive, not only at this university, but in this country. Do you understand me?" Saber was always calming people down in an amazing logical way. He was right.

"I got it. Don't worry. I'll handle it."

Saber, Ali, Karim, and Amin came over that evening. Farid had invited them for me. They tried to lift my spirits.

"Is it possible that they are spying on us? I mean in this apartment?" Farid asked while he was pouring tea for everybody.

Ali smiled. "Don't be silly. Of course not. They were snooping around us in dormitory two years ago, but our case was different."

Saber chuckled. "It is prudent to act a bit cautiously these days. Don't bring your girlfriends here… if you have any. Just in case, guys!" He chuckled.

Farid signed in a funny way. "Oh, man! You ruined my life!"

Ache crept up to my head the next day when I woke up with a stiff back. Trying not to make noise, I sneaked out without telling Farid. It was dark outside and still too early to show up at the Islamic Council, so I strolled to Azad Park, found a cosy spot between a few trees not far from the playground, and sat on a cold, moist wooden bench. Three boys in military outfits with oversized, dusty khaki backpacks on their shoulders were sluggishly walking on the north side of the park. Most probably they were in their two-year compulsory military service. Military service was compulsory for men from the age of eighteen, but I had the temporary student exemption from the military service till the end of my education. *What a waste of time*, I thought. *Such torture! The best two years of my life, working for the Islamic regime for free!*

An old lady in a black chador limped inside my cone of vision, carrying a full trolley of groceries. My eyes scanned a bunch of parsley or maybe coriander and several rods of celery sticking out of her trolley, but I hardly could see her face. The screechy sound of the trolley gradually faded away with her image on the other side of the playground. *Where did she buy those things this early in the morning?* I asked myself, standing up. Looking around, I grabbed my backpack and brushed off the dust. It was almost dawn, and the opaque moon was slowly merged on the horizon. Although it was still too early, I chose to go straight to the Council.

Not many people were in the building when I entered the reception room and asked for Mr. Haji.

"Mr. Haji is in the university mosque for morning prayer. He should be back soon. You can wait outside," the receptionist murmured while rubbing his sleepy eyes.

Wandering back to the foyer, I glanced at different announcements and photos which were hanging on both sides. Most pictures were related to the soldiers who had lost their lives in the war between Iran and Iraq. I always had a strange feeling of respect and agony for them. I hated war and despised to think about those years, but observing the faded gloomy pictures, I thought that thousands of lives could have been saved if Iran and Iraq had just not gone to war for eight bloody years. It was not pleasant at all to remember those dark days from my childhood. Nothing was pleasant in that building; nothing.

Luckily, a sudden harsh noise from the other side of the corridor brought me out of history and dumped into the current moment. It was the building janitor, a middle-aged man with a big trolley who had fallen down near the staircase. I ran to the man, took his arm, and helped him to stand up. "Are you alright? What happened?" I asked as I bent to gather his stuff from the ground.

"Oh, thank you. I was cleaning the handrails and slipped. I'm fine."

I grabbed him a glass of water from the reception room and asked if he needed any medical services?

"No. Thanks. I'm fine," he answered and drank the water. "Who are you? I've never seen you here," he said after a deep breath.

"I'm from the Engineering College. I've been called to answer some questions."

"What about?"

I smiled and replied, "Not a clue."

The man stood up, shook my hand, and said, "Thank you again. Take care."

I nodded and walked back to the reception area to put the empty glass of water on a small side table.

"Has Mr. Haji come back from the mosque?" I asked.

The receptionist glanced at me. "Yes. Wait outside. I'll call you."

I had been waiting in the corridor for more than thirty minutes when a young boy with a freshly grown beard all over his face shouted, "You! Come in!"

I walked in without saying anything and sat in a chair behind the big wooden table, the same place as last time. Mr. Haji was not in the room, but I could overhear his muffled voice from outside. A few minutes passed, and he showed up.

"Hello, Mr. Haji."

He didn't respond, just looked at me and turned his back, pretending to search for something. He was wearing a buttoned-up mandarin-collared brown shirt on top of black cotton pants. A few seconds later, he dragged a chair towards me, which made a harsh scratching noise from the friction between the posts and the floor. He sat down in front of me on the opposite side and dropped the familiar yellow folder on the table. I remembered it on the spot. He stared at me for some moments without blinking, like he was staring at a notorious criminal. I couldn't take away my eyes from the disgusting prayer bump on his forehead as I was baffled at what to do—glance back at him or ignore his filthy look?

"There are some things we cannot tolerate in this university. Neither in this place, nor in the whole city. Not only in our holy city, but also in the entire country. Can you fucking understand that?"

"Yes, I do." It slipped out of my mouth while trying to avoid saying anything more to provoke him.

"This is your Islamic Ethical Behaviour dossier. Embarrassing! You should be ashamed of yourself. I won't waste my time talking with you, anymore. You have crossed the line and put yourself in a terrible position. The decision has been made. You'll be suspended for the entire semester with the formal notice in this folder. Next time, it won't be so gentle, and you'll be treated as you deserve. Now, you can go back to your city and stay there till the next term."

He stood up and kept himself busy with other folders at the table.

I got cold feet. I was in shock, unable to react. A few seconds later, my body heated up fast and I felt sweat drip behind my head above my neck. Trying not to show any anxiety, I managed to keep myself together and muttered, "Mr. Haji, excuse me, but I do not understand. What is happening? Please explain. What did I do? What line did I cross?"

He glanced at me, sluggishly sat down again, and with an intimidating tone said, "Don't bullshit me, you piece of trash. You should've thought about it when you were talking about atheism and spitting out that nonsense about religion."

Staring at the disturbing prayer bump on his forehead, I froze and could not analyse anything for a few seconds. It seemed my brain had stopped working.

He continued, "Who asked you to say that anti-Islam crap? Who filled you up with ideas about religions like that? Whose puppet are you? Mr. Mohseni's?"

I tried to understand the circumstances and react as reasonably as possible as I remembered what Saber had told me about two choices, standing against him and telling him my true thoughts, or lying and saying whatever he wanted to hear.

"Mr. Haji, this has been a massive misunderstanding. I never said, and *will* never say, anything like that."

"So, who the hell said that he doesn't believe in any religions and God?"

"Mr. Haji, I never said that. The seminar was about Kafka's ideology, not mine. I just—"

He cut off my sentence. "Shut the hell up, you miserable piece of shit. Who the fuck is Kafka! I don't give a damn. All those nasty words were spitting from *your* filthy mouth at that ridiculous circus!" His voice echoed in the room so did in my head like a shockwave after explosion.

My whole body went absolutely numb and the only thing that I wanted to do was to escape out of that spiderweb before my blood was completely sucked out. My eyes were fixed on the table, my throat was getting dry, my lips were totally locked together, and my body stiffed like a corpse.

"Can you hear me?!" he shouted, moving closer to me.

I glanced at him and the only thing I saw was his terrifying prayer bump on his dark forehead. I desperately turned my eyes back to the table, where I noticed a paper in front of me.

"Can you hear me, I asked?!" he repeated with an annoying gesture.

I could not breathe. I was being suffocated. Something choked my throat. I hardly swallowed my saliva. "Yes."

He pushed the sheet towards me and said, "Sign it."

"What?" I didn't understand.

"Just sign it."

Glancing at the paper, I muttered, "What is it?"

"Just fucking sign it. It's a letter of commitment that you will never open your dirty mouth against God and Islam again."

"Mr. Haji, but I never *did* talk against God and Islam."

Suddenly, I remembered what Ali had told me about signing any letters. I reached for the paper and read it as fast as possible. Something was not right. It was a kind of formal confession that could prove I debated against Islam. It was also written that I was misled by Mr. Mohseni and fully regretted what I had done. Terror and suppression merged with anger and loathing, rushing through my veins, and pumping from my heart to every cell in my body. Trying to control myself, I pushed the words out dimly, "But Mr. Haji, the book seminar has nothing to do with Mr. Mohseni. I barely know him. Moreover, I didn't say any word against any religions. That was only a book review conference and had nothing to do with God or Islam."

"Who the fuck do you think you are? Huh? You are wasting my time. I can send you to jail right now."

I glanced at his face with fretful eyes and trembling lips. "Mr. Haji. Please, listen to me. It was only a usual seminar. I didn't even say the word 'Islam.' It was a general quotation on religion from someone else. Other religions, not Islam. I'm begging you. Please forgive me. Please..."

"Shut your filthy mouth. Not another word. You missed your chance."

He moved around the room, stopped near the misty window for a moment, then turned back to me and took the paper. Silently, he walked back near the window again and sat behind his desk. "Get lost! Now! You will be receiving a formal letter of suspension for the entire semester. Next time, it won't be like that. You'll be expelled permanently," he said without looking at me.

I did not even think about responding. I stood up and ran out of that callous chamber.

Being terrified, I staggered around the university complex purposelessly. My head pounded, and a vague, harsh voice was screaming inside my ears. My eyes chased the moving ground under my shoes while I took my footsteps carelessly to whatever direction they took me. My mouth was sticky, and a continuous headache was tormenting me. I had never been intimidated like that in my life. His creepy face with the abysmal prayer bump on his forehead would not get out of my mind, and his voice stormed in my head. I repeatedly heard insults and swears as if he was there with me still. I stopped, a bit dizzy, eyeing around. I was in an eerie, unfamiliar place behind the men's dormitory, an area that was filled with old, dusty trees with shredded skin hanging on from their body. A construction site was nearby, but no one was there, absolutely deserted. Teetering between the trees, I kept smashing tiny, dried branches on the ground.

A frosty wind was moving the last remaining leaves around and suspending dust and debris in the air. I stopped again and eyed around where I could see nothing but dark grey clouds, bare dried trees, and a motionless metallic structure of the half-constructed building on the gloomy horizon. My frustration and ferocity were thawing into suffocating desperation, plunging my eyes in desperate tears. I sat down on the semi-wet, dirty ground, supported my back against an old tree, covered my face with both hands, and let my torn emotions sob out of my chest. I wasn't sure how long I had been sitting there, trembling, and sobbing. It was getting dark, and I was exhausted. Shaking a bit, I tried to stand up without losing my balance.

It took forever to walk back to the dormitory. I didn't see many people in the backyard. They were probably still in classes or heading for dinner, but I was hoping to catch Ali or Saber in their room. I limped to the public toilet on the first floor and washed my face with warm water. Trying to look as normal as possible, I headed to Ali's room.

The white fluorescent lights in the hallway started to blink and turned on before I climbed the steps to the third level, faster than usual. Unexpectedly, a loud voice from the local radio station filled the entire corridor. The sound of the Azan echoed all over the building via the speakers in the ceiling. The Azan was an Arabic announcement to call everybody for praying. I stopped as soon as I heard the first sentence: "Allah o Akbar" meaning, "God is the greatest!" For the first time in my life, I suffered by hearing the Azan. A strange, devastating uproar was boiling inside me, something like a craving for revenge. I could feel the powerful urge to destruct. I remembered everything from my childhood, like a terrifying short movie, scene by scene, all those years of brainwashing by Islamic media, Islamic society, and Islamic schools. I remembered that my sixth grade Islamic Theology teacher lectured while systematically sowing the seeds of superstitious thoughts in students' brains. "All Muslims will eventually fly to the wonderful eternal paradise and the rest of the people will be burnt in blazing flames of the most terrifying hell." We were only thirteen years old.

The Azan was still dispatching from the radio and my brain could not stop flipping through snapshots from those days. The deeper I thought, the more I detested the whole concept of religion. It was an insane pivotal moment. One of those first times in life which cannot be forgotten.

I was locked into my thoughts when I realised that someone was shaking me. "Are you alright? Nima? Where the hell have you been? Nima?!" Jalal was talking to me while his hands were on my shoulders, trying to catch my attention.

I looked at him with half-open mouth like I wanted to say something but couldn't find the right words. "Um… I'm fine. Um… I don't know. No, I'm not okay. I'm not fine."

"Shit, your eyes are bloody red. Come on man, let's go." He gently pushed me towards Ali's room. "Let's go inside. We were worried about you, pal."

Everybody was there, Ali, Farid, Saber, Amin, and Karim. Looking at their familiar faces, I forgot my headache.

"He is here!" Jalal shouted.

"Where have you been all day? Your face is pale!" Farid yelled, and asked Ali to pour me a cup of tea. "Okay, okay, sit down," Farid continued.

"We were so worried. We looked everywhere for you," Ali whispered while giving me a warm mug.

Muttering words and broken sentences came out of my dried mouth disorderly. Drinking the hot tea, I somehow managed to vaguely explain what had happened as much as I could.

Saber eyed Ali. "I knew it. I told you!" Then he continued, "Everything is going to be alright. This isn't the first time they are playing this card."

Ali added, "Saber and I were summoned there several times. They told us the exact same thing."

I stared at them. "What thing? That moron suspended me."

Ali replied, "Chill out. He cannot suspend you like that. He must officially report you to HR, and then *they* will review the allegation. They have to interview you again, and then make a decision."

I moved a bit to adjust my back against the wall so I could bring down the ache in my spine. Trying to control my temper, I replied, "Come on, man. I'm very well aware of *Starred Students*. I know, and you know better than me, that the Islamic Council easily sacks 'Starred Students' without reporting to any authority. You know that. All of us know that. They put a star mark near your name in their system, in the bloody Islamic Ethical Behaviour folder, and then expel you. So why are you rubbing salt in my wound?"

There was a moment of discomforting silence in the room. Saber dragged himself closer.

Ali also came and sat in front of me. "I'm not saying everything is going well, and I'm certainly not trying to rub salt in anyone's wound. We're all together in this."

Saber added, "Ali is a starred student. He was suspended two years ago. They sent him home in his fourth semester

because he was running a petition for freedom of speech—
nothing against Islam or any other rules. They also disqualified
him from all student activities during his education. This is
why he is not a member of any student organization."

Jalal moved near the window. "You are right, Nima. They
don't need any official reporting or even any evidence. They
do whatever they want. But keep in mind that we are trying
to change this situation as much as possible. We have to! We
must! Three years back, and I mean it, only three years ago,
who would've thought that someone could question the Basij's
policy and challenge them? Let alone present an ideological
conference against religious mindsets. You do realize how
difficult it was for all of us to get to this point? Every single
step we took was extremely tough and painful. This is our life
we are talking about."

I listened without blinking.

Saber put his hand on my shoulder. "We will go and talk
with Mr. Haji tomorrow. It was very wise of you that you
didn't sign that bloody letter. I have a buddy in the School of
Literature. He can help us, too. He knows Mr. Haji very well.
Leave it with us for now."

CHAPTER 8

ooking around with half-closed, swollen eyes, I barely dragged myself out of the bed; my bare feet tingled on the chilled floor. Farid had already left for the university but luckily, I didn't have a morning class. A bit wobbly, I headed to the bathroom, spun the hot water faucet, stood aside for a few seconds till the water warmed up enough. I stared at the frameless mirror on the wall. *Why am I here? Why? We live and we die! Is that it?* Steam gradually covered the mirror and I saw nothing but an opaque, trembling shadow. *Sooner or later, want it or not, we all die and turn to dust. What a ridiculous life!*

It was almost lunchtime when I left my apartment. I shielded my eyes with my hand and looked at the sky where a couple of fluffy sparrows were chasing each other near a fat unbalanced tree just outside the window of the first floor. I didn't notice many cars on the streets and there were only a few people around. It was a sunny day, but I felt a thin layer of frosty air on my nose as I glanced up to the trees, staring at the naked branches, and walked to the college a different way than usual. Passing along the quiet alleys, I reached Shahid Boulevard and headed to the telephone centre, which was not on my way to the university. Entering the building, I handed over a phone number to a drowsy receptionist and waited aside. No one was there at that time, and he called my name in less than a minute: "Mr. Zarin. Cabin One."

I entered the cabin. Picking up the receiver, I heard the call had not gone through yet. *Pick up. Pick up the phone, please.* It kept ringing on the other end of the line.

"Hello?" the most familiar voice in the world answered.

"Hi, Mom. How are you?" I didn't tell her anything about the last few days. I just wanted to hear her voice and picture myself there, in my home.

It was about one o'clock when I arrived at the university, hoping to see Taban as I simply needed her. The bus service was passing by University Boulevard and a dusty white car was trying to overtake it. I walked faster and headed to the Cultural Unit to find Taban. She wasn't there. No one was there. *Maybe she is in the library or dormitory? Where are the others? Ali and Saber? They probably went to the canteen,* I guessed. The door was open, but I didn't wait, and walked towards the café to eat something.

"Hey, Nima. How are you doing? Saber was looking for you," Abbas said.

"Hi, Abbas. Do you know when? He wasn't at the Unit."

"Half an hour ago. He saw me in the corridor and asked if I had caught you up."

"Um, okay. Maybe he's at the canteen for lunch. Thanks!"

"Any time, buddy. See you in an hour! Don't forget. It'll be an important subject today. You don't want to mess with the thermodynamics class, do you?"

I didn't answer. *What's the point? I am suspended.*

Abbas insisted, "Sure?"

"Yes, pal. See you in an hour."

What did Saber want to tell me? Please be good news. Is it possible that he somehow sorted out the issue already? I was flicking through different thoughts in my mind. "Your sandwich is ready!" I grabbed my lunch and almost ran back to the Cultural Unit. Still, no one was there. I sat behind the table, glanced at the random photos around, ate my sandwich, and for a moment, everything slipped away from my head. Occasionally, some noises from outside caught my attention. I glanced at the door, hoping to see Taban, Saber or Ali. I tore an inch of the paper wrapped around the sandwich and took another bite, then I turned my head around the room, where a thick book with a bending cover on the bookshelf near the door caught my eye. It was laid on the shelf instead of in a vertical position like the other books. Grabbing another piece of my sandwich, I stepped closer to the bookcase to see the book. It was *Freedom or Death* by Nikos Kazantzakis. Flipping the pages, I remembered the days when I had read it and talked with my father about Captain Michalis, his ideology, and what he chose at last. Putting the book upright in the bookcase, I heard someone called me.

"Hi, man. You are here. How are you today? Feeling better?" Jalal asked me while he dropped a pack of magazines on the table.

"Not bad. Thanks. Have you seen Saber? Abbas told me he was looking for me," I said impatiently.

Jalal kept tidying up the table. "No, but I know he went to the Council this morning to discuss your situation. He went with Karim. Maybe they are at the canteen for lunch or—" He had not finished his sentence when Saber and Karim walked into the room. They looked weary as if someone brushed their faces with fatigue and frustration.

We shook hands and I couldn't wait to ask what had happened. "Did you see Mr. Haji? How did it go? What happened?"

Saber sat near the window and Karim closed the door.

I dragged a chair towards Saber. "So?"

"Do you want the good news first or the bad news?"

"I had enough bad news yesterday. Start with the good news, please."

"We reached the agreement with the Islamic Council not to suspend you."

"Really?! This is awesome, pal. Thank you. Thank you!" I was so relieved that I did not let Saber continue his words. I stood up and marched around the table. Then stopped near the bookcase, looked at Saber, and asked, "How?"

"You need to give them a formal commitment."

"Commitment? What for?"

"They want a written commitment that you do not talk against Islam in any possible way."

"Isn't it the same confession letter that I refused to sign yesterday?"

"Um… not really, um… it's different. It is not unusual for them to get commitments and put restrictions on students, but this one is a bit open to interpretation."

"What do you mean?"

"They can link everything to it." He paused and cleared his throat. "Think about it. You talk about equality between men and women, they will find something against Islam in it. Debate on modernism, socialism, ethics, government, privacy, family, anything—they will connect it somehow to governmental Islamic rules. Chat about eating fast food? They will find a way to reference it to religion. Got it?"

I was trying to follow him, word by word. His concern was valid. That was how the tyrannies kept themselves alive. Shaking my head agitatedly, I said, "I understand. But do I have another choice?"

"I don't know. There won't be anything about Mr. Mohseni in the commitment letter, though. Maybe still risky to sign it, but then..."

"And then what?"

"But then, you need to follow your gut. Who gives a shit what they are asking? They have all the power and force everybody to do exactly what they want, anyway."

"I agree. At least I can dodge the bullet till the next one. It is better than wasting an entire term. So… was that the bad news? The commitment?"

"Not quite," said Karim.

"Oh, boy. Tell me everything."

Saber continued, "They shut the literature club down."

"What?"

"No more book debates or meetings or anything like that."

"What the fuck!?"

"They said these events can easily deviate from Islamic principles, which is what allegedly happened."

Karim grimaced and looked at me. "We always find another way. They shut this door, we build another door. Even larger!"

Jalal added, "Like these!" He pointed to the bunch of journals on the table.

"What about them?" I asked.

He grabbed one of the magazines. "They ceased publishing the Cultural Unit magazine two years ago because Ali wrote a political article criticizing the system. The article implied a corrupted government and how that impacted students at universities. It was so true that they could not argue with it. They banned us from writing political articles within the Unit and revoked the permit to publish the journal. The lame excuse was that the Unit had to deal with cultural events, not advertising personal political views. Three months after that, we decided to publish a new journal. Here we are now!"

The next day, I signed the commitment letter. A commitment I never kept.

CHAPTER 9

I

"Two years have gone by," said Farid with a cheerful tone and a genuine smile on his face while we were heading to the library to study for the final exams.

I answered joyfully when we reached the library, "Almost, yes. Halfway through!"

Taban was near the men's entrance, waiting for me as I'd missed a couple tutorials and had asked for her thermodynamics notebook.

"Thanks, Taban. I'll bring it back to you this afternoon."

She raised her hands as if she was lecturing us, stared at me and Farid, and said, "Don't worry about it. The last session was all practicing on different questions. I wrote them all. I think you haven't missed that much. Anyway, Farid was in the class, too. Ask him if you can't read my handwriting!"

Her eyes sparkled as she winked at Farid.

Farid stared at me and said, "Did you hear that? You could've asked me in the first place! Why did you ask for Miss Pakzad's notebook?"

Laughing together, we went to the men's study area and Taban walked to the women's section. Looking for a free spot, I found Abbas and Reza at the far end of the salon near the window which was protected by bronze bars from outside.

"Hi, guys. What are you up to?" I asked them and adjusted a chair slightly away from their desk.

Abbas smiled and whispered, "We're studying thermodynamics for the final exam."

I stared at him. "Final exam? Come on, folks. Wrap it up. Let's get out of here. What about swimming pool and sauna?"

They all turned their heads. "Shut up and sit down."

We all burst into quiet laughter and then I took out my stuff from my backpack and set them on my desk.

"That's not yours. That is Miss Pakzad's notebook. I knew it!" Abbas said, grinning.

"Hush! I'm studying." I smirked and opened the textbook while glancing at Taban's notebook. Flicking through the pages, I tried to memorize the important formulas and associated equations. Looking at some examples, I began to resolve them on my own. Reviewing different chapters, I reached the middle of the book.

"Gibbs Energy, my favourite topic of all time," I said out loud.

Farid angled his head towards me and whispered, "What?"

I had been researching this subject for several months and the more I dug into it, the deeper I fell in love with it. I paused and turned on my chair, a bit excited as the Gibbs Theory wasn't just a fundamental thermodynamics concept to me. I snapped my fingers. "Folks. Listen to me."

Abbas, Reza and Farid gazed at me.

I continued in a low tone like I was deciphering a secret plan, "Listen, listen. Have you comprehended that the Gibbs Theory is a life-changing ideology? Our functionality is entirely being controlled by Gibbs Energy."

Abbas and Farid gave me a surprised look and asked together, "What do you mean?"

I dragged my chair closer to them and answered, "It proves that the smaller the level of energy between two substances, the stronger the connections between their molecules. It means AB has less Gibbs Energy than A and B individually."

Abbas stared at me without any reaction.

Reza joined us and asked, "What the hell are you talking about? Of course, AB has less Gibbs Energy than its own components. AB has already reached the chemical equilibrium state."

I nodded my head and snapped my fingers. "Bang on! Mr. A sees Miss B, and they feel something mutual, um… something like a magnetic vibe, unavoidable desire to bond. After some time, they become closer to each other and fall in love. The AB has less amount of Gibbs Energy than Mr. A or Miss B on their own. So, they're being forced by nature to be the AB family."

Farid leaned forward and said, "Correct. This is the basic thermodynamics law. You just turned it into a romantic anecdote."

"But it makes sense, doesn't it?" I replied, waiting for the confirmation.

They twitched their mouth and nodded.

I continued with slightly more excitement in my voice, "Very well! Now," I paused for a second. "*Now*, imagine Miss C approaches the happily-ever-after AB. Miss C is sneaking into their life. Is it possible that Mr. A splits up with his wife and starts a new life with Miss C?" I narrowed my eyes and grinned. "It is, indeed! The lower level of Gibbs Energy would do the job, right?"

Reza hummed while Abbas and Farid stared at me without saying a word.

"Miss C is now near the AB family. The level of Gibbs Energy between Mr. A and Miss C is lower than the energy between Mr. A and his wife. According to this theory, in this situation, the AB family will be separated, and the new couple takes place with a lower Gibbs level. It means Mr. A will divorce Miss B and joins Miss C. The new couple will be AC and Miss B will be alone again."

Farid scratched his head with a half-open mouth and Reza's eyes were fixed on my face. "Interesting!" was the only word they said.

I kept going. "Does this mean we don't have choices in our life? Or we are forced to react according to the situation? Look around yourselves! People are falling in love, getting married, and then everything becomes normal, and they leave each other for a new man or woman. Do human relationships function per the Gibbs Theory? Does every relationship need protection against Miss C or Mr. D? It is scientifically proven that the lower the Gibbs Energy, the stronger the bond! So, the question is: how can we find a partner with the lowest level of Gibbs Energy? This will guarantee the strongest relationship. That would be the real love. Isn't it amazing!?"

Farid and Abbas glanced at each other, winked, and simultaneously twirled their finger near their ears, whispering, "Cuckoo!"

We all continued studying till lunchtime and left the library together. They went to the canteen, and I headed to find Taban to return her notebook. Thinking about the final exams, I noted a new announcement related to the Tehran protest on the Cultural Unit's board. I was aware about the content but hadn't guessed that Saber was going to pin it on the board. I paused for some minutes and glanced around at a few other students reading the announcement. It was more like a piece of informative news rather than an announcement.

Tehran University had boycotted their final exams because the Science Ministry had forbidden two students from academic education for the rest of their lives. Saber had reliable information from the capital that the Ministry of Intelligence had ordered the dismissal, and an anonymous judge charged those students with incitement against national security. Several universities in the country, including ours, had started a petition to reverse the verdict and planned for another demonstration.

"It is unbearable," said Ali from the other corner.

"Sadly," I replied.

He glanced at the board again. "Yes, we must speed up. It's been two days, and no one took any responsibility. Authorities don't answer any questions. They just sacked those students. I personally knew them. They wanted more freedom and less censorship at the university."

Walking towards the Cultural Unit, Ali explained more. He was talking firm and clear as usual, with a short pause between each sentence till we reached the Unit.

Ali checked on a calendar that was hanging adjacent to the bookcase. "The University of Tehran Cultural Unit has formally asked HR to chase the issue, but they ignored the request. They also officially sent two letters to the university headquarters and the Science Ministry office, but there has been no answer even now. It is terrifying."

I strolled around the table, thinking about how stressful the situation could be for them. "So, what's gonna happen next?"

"As you know, we'll start the protest soon. Saber has another meeting this afternoon with our team in other colleges, and then we'll make a decision on how to proceed."

"I understand, but do we have enough time? Soon will be our final exams."

"I'm aware of it," Ali paused as he was thinking about the next sentence, but he didn't continue.

A round clock on the wall on top of the door showed two o'clock and it was then when I realized that I'd forgotten to give Taban her notebook back. I said goodbye to Ali and raced out of the room. Almost jogging towards the café, I saw one of her friends and our classmate near the back door.

"Have you seen Miss Pakzad? Is she in the café?"

The answer was short and quick. "No."

I walked back and went up to the computer room. *She might be there,* I hoped. Entering the computer room, I couldn't find her there, but found Abbas and two of our classmates. I approached them and asked the same question.

"She was here an hour ago when we came back from the canteen. Maybe she went for a late lunch," Abbas answered.

I marched out guessing other places where she might be. We didn't have any classes for the rest of the day, and I had promised to give her back her notebook by lunchtime. *Shit. What should I do now? Would it be a good idea if I go to her apartment and give it back?* The thought landed on me tenderly like an innocent temptation. I had accompanied her many times to her place, but never had a chance to walk inside. *Should I call her first? Not now, better to call her when I get close to her place.* I was pretty sure she would say, "Oh, no rush, you could give it back tomorrow." But I didn't want that. I was eager to meet her in a private place, neither in the university nor in a restaurant or café. So, I walked out of the university, took a shortcut to Abad Boulevard, and waved my hand for a passing cab, hoping Taban would be at her place. It was a scorching, sunny day. Trying to waggle my backpack and get some air movement underneath, I spotted a car stopped a couple of meters farther and a passenger took off from it. I ran to the cab, jumped in, and said, "Straightaway to the middle of Abad Boulevard."

The driver nodded and shifted the manual gear. All four windows were rolled down and hot wind was hitting my face from all directions like a gigantic hair dryer set on high. Sky-high trees on both sides of the street blurred past by while a piece of lazy cloud with the shape of a cauliflower heavily dragged itself on the horizon. It wasn't rush hour, so I arrived in less than five minutes. Thrilled to meet Taban, I paid the fare to the driver and got out in a rush. Looking around, I walked to the opposite side of the street, squeezed into the yellow public telephone cabin, and shut the heavy metal accordion door. "Oh, boy! Is this a phone cabin or a public dry sauna?" I nagged under my breath, dropped in a coin, and dialled. My hands trembled a bit as I heard the connection ring on the phone, and in a second my heart began to beat faster. It was like I was planning for my first date with Taban. I couldn't stand the stifling cabin and tried to open the door with my foot while I hung on to the receiver.

"Hello?" I couldn't tell if it was Taban or her roommate.

"Hello. I'd like to talk with Taban, please."

"Nima? Is that you?" Taban answered.

"Hi, yes. Yes. How are you?"

"Very well. Thanks. Is everything alright?"

"Um. Yes. Just wanted to know if you are at home. I'm so sorry, I forgot to give your notebook back."

"That's fine. Don't worry about it."

"Actually, I'm near your place."

"What? You've got to be kidding me."

"I just wanted to see if it's okay for you that I bring it over?"

"Of course. You always surprise me. Ring flat number zero when you arrive. I'm waiting."

A few minutes later, I was in front of her place, a three-story white building on a quiet, narrow street with more than a few mulberry trees opposite the doorway. I pressed her unit number on the intercom and the door opened without anyone asking anything. For a few seconds, I was confused. *Should I wait? Should I sneak in? What should I do?* Taban's voice from the speaker ended my bewilderment, "Come on in. Take the steps and walk down to the underground unit." I'd heard what she said, but my foot did not move at all. It was the very first time we would be alone together, far from any other eyes. We had never met in her apartment or my place. My heart was about to race out of my chest. I took a deep breath and stepped past the gate.

Looking down at the newly washed stairs, I saw Taban, leaning against the door frame. Her alluring, dark, long hair was like a silky waterfall that complemented her deep, vibrant, black eyes. She waved her naked hand and quietly said, "Come on in." I hesitated for a few seconds. She picked up my pause and quickly added, "Hey, don't be shy. Come on in."

"I'm not shy." I chuckled, took off my shoes and went inside. "This is a beautiful, cosy apartment."

"Thanks. Tea, juice, water?" She wore an orange gypsy skirt and a white tank top with no socks. My eyes swiftly brushed past her red polished toenails and then fixed on her face.

"Are you alone?" I asked while she stepped into the kitchen to pour tea.

"Yes. My roomie has already finished her semester and went back to her city," Taban almost shouted from the kitchen.

I sat on a small sofa and took out her notebook from my backpack, leaving it on the small brown coffee table in the centre of the room near an empty crystal vase. I still felt my chest bouncing up and down.

Taban came out with two cups of tea on a small silver tray, carefully laid the tray on the coffee table and sat in a tiny armchair near the sofa. Glancing at her notebook near the vase, she asked, "Ready for the exam?"

I took a drink of my tea. "I hope so! Thanks for the notebook."

She smiled and leaned forward to take her tea from the table. Her wavy hair slid along her shoulder and slipped in front of her chest, stopping just on top of her voluptuous breasts.

My breath came out of my mouth in an unusually difficult way. It was like something hot and heavy was pressed to my chest. My hands couldn't move without a tiny shaking in my arms. I changed my head's direction as fast as I could and squirmed on the sofa. My body reactions were out of my control. I took another sip and stood up.

"I have to go. Lots of things to do. Thanks for the tea."

"What? At least finish your tea." A bit surprised, she chuckled.

Dragging myself to the door, I muttered, "Um, I truly enjoyed our moments. We should see each other more. Um, I mean, outside of the university. I mean, like today."

"Like today? Just a few minutes?" she grinned.

"I mean…"

Taban laughed and cut my words. "I know what you mean. Sure. Absolutely. I'd love to." She paused and gazed at me for a few seconds before I put on my shoes, and then whispered, "Do you want my notebook again?"

II

A few days later, I visited Abbas and Reza in the dormitory to study for the final exams together. Farid had made plans to play tennis with Amin and then join us afterward. A group of students were standing outside the entrance when I arrived at the dormitory. It wasn't unusual that some folks hung out and smoked, but something was not right as they were talking in a rush and moving around like they were looking for something. The voices were getting louder as I crossed the entrance and headed to the third floor, a bit curious. Some doors were left open, and boys were almost running to the end of the corridor where Saber and Ali's room was located. I sped up and asked the first person on my way, "What's happening?" He didn't hear what I asked and passed me in haste, changing my curiosity to an eerie feeling. I looked around perplexed and darted to Ali's room. The door was open, and I saw unfamiliar faces inside the room before stepping in. Jalal was near the window, talking with a man I didn't know.

"What's happened? Where are Ali and Saber?" I asked anxiously.

Jalal glanced at me. His face was pale. "They took them early this morning."

"What? What do you mean? Who took them? Where?"

"We don't know. It was about seven o'clock. Some men broke into the dorm and took them, um… not only Ali and Saber. It seems they caught several students from other colleges."

"Oh, no. Why?"

"We don't know yet. They don't need a reason!" he said in anger.

I eyed around as confusion and fear rapidly grew inside me. Whatever it was, I could not stop it.

"What should we do now? Have you called the police?" I asked.

"Yes, we did. We also informed the Dean."

"And?"

"And what? What do you expect? We've been told that they would take care of the situation. This means they knew about it. Meaning those pricks don't give a shit." Jalal's lips trembled.

The man near Jalal said, "We're heading to the university headquarters now. Let's go."

Jalal bit his lips again and shook his head.

I asked, "Why are we going there?"

The other man answered, "We have no choice but to gather and start a demonstration in front of the headquarters. We've already informed the other colleges. They'll join us to escalate the situation. The unknown agents literally kidnapped our friends. We can't waste our time sitting here. We must do something."

We left the dormitory building and stormed to the university headquarters, which was not far from the Faculty of Science. Getting closer to the building, we saw that some students had already gathered in front of the doorway.

"That's what I'd expected," Jalal murmured.

"What? The crowd?" I asked, breathing heavily as it was getting hot. Jalal didn't hear me and moved faster towards the headquarters. The crowd was gradually growing. Looking around in disbelief, I spotted Karim with his roommate near the entrance.

I walked towards him and asked, "How long you've been here?"

His face was covered with a layer of sweat and wet spots were steadily growing between his armpits. "We've been here since eight o'clock. They locked the gate and no one from the headquarters is coming out. They said the university president is out on a business trip. Bullshit!"

I tried to look inside the building but couldn't see anything as sunlight's reflection transformed the closed glassy door to a blurry mirror.

"Any news from Saber and Ali? Did anyone find out where they are?" I asked without expecting to receive a positive answer.

Karim wiped his forehead with a tissue and said, "No. They didn't let us to go inside till ten minutes ago, when two of us headed to the main office. Now we're waiting till they show up."

While Karim was talking, I noted that two men with cameras near the parking area, far from the crowd, were filming. I looked over Karim's shoulder and whispered, "Who are they?"

"I don't know, maybe from the Islamic Council, maybe from the Basij Organization. They've been here since early morning."

"I'm sure some guys from outside of the university are here, too. Look at them. They aren't students." I pointed to a group of men with long beards who were noiselessly standing far from the crowd watching everybody.

"No, they aren't. Those pricks might even provoke others to do stupid things. Sometimes they create problems, you know—violence, breaking windows..."

The crowd was progressively expanding as girls and boys joined the gathering one after another. I tried to find Jalal, but could not see him anywhere around.

We'd been waiting under a blazing, sunny sky for about two hours. The area was full of students from different colleges; some of them had to stand near the parking area or a bit farther away. Walking among them, I heard something happening in front of the headquarters' entrance. The core of the crowd began to move towards the building. It was getting denser as the crowd pressed each other to get closer so they could see what was happening. Pushing the fellows around, I crept inch by inch to the centre of the crowd and spotted Jalal with two men who were certainly older than him. Karim was a few meters farther, standing near the building's east wall. I squeezed myself among a group of boys in the centre of the yard, opened my way between the crowd, and walked towards him. "What's happening?"

Karim stared at the gate. "The two students, who went in to talk with the uni authorities, just showed up. Can you see them? Jalal is now talking with them."

The humming noise from each corner became louder as almost all the students were talking together, curious, and, in some cases, furious.

"Everybody, please listen up!" shouted the oldish man who was talking with Jalal earlier.

Karim craned his neck near my ears and almost yelled, "He's the leader of the Faculty of Science Cultural Unit!"

I looked back to the main entrance where the leader was trying to deliver a message. Although he was shouting, we couldn't hear him very well. "We are here to defend our fundamental rights. Listen to me, please!" The roaring noise slowly disappeared like an ocean wave sliding on shore. He continued, "Five of our classmates, our friends, have been taken out by force from their rooms this morning. We believe that they've been arrested by Intelligence Ministry agents. I've just had a discussion with the university president. As we expected, he denied government involvement." He paused for a second as a dry cough cut his words. "The uni president claimed he was not aware of anything unusual; however, he issued an order to investigate the so-called incident. Shame on them!" He tried to shout louder while his hand hovered above his head. "We want the truth. We want our friends back. No one has the right to raid the dorm and capture our classmates. The university is a protected area. There are checkpoints everywhere, from the entrance gates to each dorm and all colleges. How's it possible that some unknown agents drove in with a van, entered the complex without any permit, came to the dorm, and kidnapped our friends without any problem?"

The more he talked, the more noises and movements came from the crowd. I could see the melange of anger and excitement everywhere. He tried to speak louder but his dried throat didn't let him say anything more. "We do not leave until we get our friends back. We are peacefully demanding the immediate release of our roommates. We are students, not criminals. This is a university, not a military camp. We want freedom. This is our first and foremost right!"

He paused for a second and the crowd started shouting, "Freedom! Freedom! Freedom!"

He walked closer to the centre and yelled, "Freedom! Freedom!"

Everybody repeated, "Freedom! Freedom!"

I spotted more cameras around filming everybody from different angles and that was when I lost my temper and angrily shouted, "What are you recording? Why are you filming?"

Some students glanced at me and then turned to the cameras. Another guy from the crowd yelled, "Take the cameras. They aren't students. Get them all!"

In the blink of an eye, a group of five or six from the crowd ran to the cameramen. The cameramen stepped back a couple of meters and tried to escape, but the students caught up with them, broke the cameras, took the films out, and destroyed them all. Someone shouted, "Keep calm! Don't get physical! Just films! Keep calm!" But it was too late as the cameramen and some other folks had started to fight. Struggling to keep my distance, I saw one of the cameramen trying to barge out of the area by pushing everybody to the left and right. He jumped towards me and for a few seconds our gaze merged. He did not hesitate and pushed me aside, running to the other side of the building. His face was so familiar. I was pretty sure I had seen him somewhere. I rapidly scanned my memories. Clenching my fist, I realized who he was. "Holy fuck!" I shouted towards him. He was the janitor who I had helped at the Islamic Council building several months back. I tried to find him, but it was too late as he had disappeared. It was obvious that some other intruders were inside the student gathering. The fight escalated fast and most of those in the crowd, intentional or not, got somehow involved.

Suddenly, the intrusive screeching sounds of motorcycle tires against asphalt filled the air and before I could put my hands over my ears, six black motorcycles with two or three passengers drove in front of the doorways and fully geared militia forces in black outfits jumped into the central yard. Hard metallic batons soared on their hands and landed on students before anyone could react. A rough, scratchy voice from a hand loudspeaker frequently repeated, "Leave the area now. Do not stay here. Leave the area immediately." They hit us and began to arrest some students. Boys and girls tried to find a way to escape. The armed forces were not supposed to be allowed to enter the university, but no one understood how they had gotten inside.

Jalal shouted at one of the guarded militias while another armed man approached him from behind with a long black baton. I stepped forward and screamed, "Leave him alone. Jalal, run!" Three muscular students noticed, as well, and jumped towards Jalal to protect him. The militiaman backed off as the bulky students reached Jalal. I struggled to move as a group of students tried to run and blocked the way. "Jalal!" I shouted again, "Let's go, this way!"

Jalal joined me and we ran behind the Faculty of Science building and exited the university as fast as we could. We were both sweating, shaking, and a bit disoriented. Jalal was stumbling with a pain in his hips, as he had been hit by a baton. We limped along University Boulevard to the main street, took a cab, and headed to my place.

We entered the apartment and threw ourselves on the sofa.

"Are you okay?" I asked Jalal out of breath.

"Yes. I'm fine."

After a few minutes, I stood up, still dizzy, washed my face, and asked, "What should we do now? What's gonna happen?"

Jalal was still sitting on the sofa, trying to check on his back wound. "We'll go to the dorm. We must get to the bottom of this shit. We can't sit and do nothing."

We were in shock and couldn't take a nap or even close our eyes. We just laid motionless on the sofa and gazed at the blank roof. I whispered, "When anger and anxiety combine with fear and suppression, your throat gets dry, and your tongue cannot spit a word out. Your mind is unable to handle mixed messages from your brain, and it all leaves you no choice but to stare at the invisible space behind your dark loneliness. You will endlessly suffer from what you have no control over." I slowly turned back to Jalal, gazing at him. He was sleeping; or maybe I was sleeping.

It took more than an hour before we had almost recovered from the shock and numbness of what had happened at the university.

"How are you feeling, buddy? Getting better?" I asked Jalal while I was trying to stand up.

"Don't know. Let's go to the dorm."

I changed my sweaty shirt, and we left the apartment. It was still daylight. We stopped at Abad Boulevard to take a cab. Our eyes unintentionally pursued all the passing cars, buses, and motorcycles that rumbled past. I took out a tissue and mopped a thin layer of warm sweat from my face and neck.

"What time is it?" I asked Jalal.

"No idea," he answered, and then glanced at his watch. "Almost four o'clock."

In the dusty, stuffy cab, we tried to figure out how that chaos had happened and why.

When we arrived at the dormitory, I didn't see anyone in front of the entrance hall. Heading inside, I found the corridor just like other normal days—some students were walking around with their pyjamas, some doors were open to circulate the air, and often I heard music inside rooms. We headed straight to Ali's room, where we found no one, and then rushed to Karim's place, one floor above. Approaching his room, we could hear people talking loudly inside. We knocked and entered.

Karim stood up. "Where have you been? We were worried about you."

Jalal answered, "We ran off to Nima's place."

"I guessed so."

"What the hell happened to your forehead?" I asked Karim as I stared at a walnut-sized bruise on the top of his left eyebrow.

"Nothing. I got injured by one of those assholes. The guy near me got hit on the head and injured badly."

"Assholes!" I said aggressively. "You'll be fine!" The room was busy with different students, and I knew most of them. "Any news from Ali and Saber?" I asked quietly.

"Yes," Karim answered. "Most probably they are at the Islamic Council. Naser told us." He pointed to a man in a brown long-sleeved shirt who was standing near the window, drinking water from a small plastic bottle.

He was probably in his forties or older. Naser was an old friend of Karim's father. He worked in the central library, and he had some connections inside the Council.

Naser nodded his head. "They've been holding them in the building, in separate rooms for interrogation."

Jalal vexed, "Interrogation?"

Naser continued, "Maybe they will be released before night."

I glanced at him and asked, "How do you know?"

He smiled bitterly. "Just a wild guess. Believe me, I wouldn't know anything about them if the Islamic Council wanted to make them disappear. A guy in reception simply told me the students were kept in separate rooms for questioning. It means they didn't send them out of the university, and they won't. Especially after what happened today in front of the headquarters."

Jalal sat near the window and took a couple of deep breaths. "This is good news. Hopefully the Council releases them soon."

Karim approached Jalal and said, "You are pale like fuck. Are you injured, buddy?"

I answered, "No, nothing important, but we haven't eaten anything since morning. Let's go to the café."

Karim looked at his watch. "The dorm's canteen will open for dinner soon. Let's go there. Come on."

He patted Jalal's back while Naser said goodbye and left the room. We headed to the restaurant a few minutes later, after Jalal took a quick shower and put on clean clothes. It was getting dark outside, and a warm, gentle wind was blowing that roasting day away. Karim said, "I'm a bit relaxed now. I'm sure the Ministry of Intelligence agents did not take them somewhere unknown. This is a relief. Hope they come back soon."

Jalal responded, "Fingers crossed."

We entered the quiet canteen as if nowhere else to go and nothing else to do.

It was almost nine o'clock at night when Ali and Saber showed up with puffy eyes, dried lips, and wrinkled faces. Their shirts were wet, and their pants were stained from sweat. They didn't talk a lot and we did not ask too much, just ensured they were fine and had no physical injuries. The Ministry of Intelligence agents had interrogated them for more than five hours. Five straight hours of intimidation, insult, and mental torture. The focus was on the Tehran protest and any plan related to it for our university.

"You are exhausted, you must rest. We'll leave you alone. Alright?" I winked at Karim and the other guys in the room. We all said goodbye and headed out.

The next day, I found out Ali had been expelled from the university during his last semester and banned from continuing any academic education in the future. Saber had been suspended till next semester. He was not allowed to attend final exams and automatically failed the whole semester.

CHAPTER 10

I

One week had passed since Ali's dismissal, and it was such a shock to every one of us. Most of the courses had already finished and it was the countdown time for the final exams. As the university was getting quieter, it was more challenging to get support for the protest. Although Saber was suspended for the entire semester, he didn't leave the city. He was continuously in touch with other colleges to join the integrated protest around the whole country, a nationwide demonstration within all universities. The date had been set for the day after the last exam. Tehran University was leading the movement, and they had released an invitation to all students around the country to join the demonstration.

I was frequently in touch with Saber for the latest update, but as the academic year was about to end, I'd been trying to focus on my final exams by spending more time with Abbas, Farid, and Reza. Sometimes, we gathered to review our lessons in the library, and the other times, in the dormitory.

A couple of days before the first exam, Farid and I headed to the dormitory to study with the other folks, ask various questions and solve some samples from the previous year's tests. It had been a long, blistering day with no sign of cooling down and it wasn't easy to keep our eyes open after lunch. It was like the atmosphere had been infused with soothing sleeping agents.

"We should've come in the morning. I'm getting dizzy in this weather. I want to lie down right now and take a nap exactly under the shadow of that tree!" I told Farid, not far from the dormitory. Walking inside, I saw Jalal with a takeaway food bag in his hand. He was strolling back to his room from the canteen. "You go, I'll join you soon," I told Farid, and ran towards Jalal.

"Any news from Ali? Have you called him recently?" I asked, a bit out of breath.

"Yes, he's still trying to get over it. He was considering the immigration option. Getting out of the country."

"It makes sense. He can't continue his education. It is very difficult to lose everything after four years of studying. Moreover, he's unable to find a decent job in this condition."

Talking about the other students who were expelled from the university last week, we entered Jalal's room. Karim and Saber were there. I paused a bit upon entering the room, my mouth half-open, as I had not expected them to be there.

"What's going on, guys?" I asked, sitting near the window to get some fresh air.

"Rumour has it that several universities in Tehran, Tabriz, and Isfahan are preparing to boycott the final exams," Saber said.

"Oh, boy! No way!"

"Last night I had a chat with Ali over the phone. His friends at Tehran University believed that one option to send our message louder is by boycotting the exams."

"Oh, man! Unlikely to happen! I really doubt if the majority of students would support the idea. You know what I'm talking about. Moreover, it is too late. The first exam will be the day after tomorrow."

"Yes. Not many are willing to take this risk. And there's not enough time to organize such a crucial protest. It's a huge step and needs everybody's support."

Jalal continued, "The Ministry of Intelligence created an atmosphere filled with fear and stress. They heard about the nationwide protest at the end of the semester and began to call the leaders and interrogate students, anyone who was showing any interest in supporting the movement." He smirked, "Yesterday, they summoned me to the Islamic Council, but I didn't show up! I think it pissed them off. They just want to control the university till the semester is over. Then everybody will be leaving for the summer holidays."

Saber sat on the floor and leaned back against the bed, puffing a short sigh out. He stretched his leg and said, "This isn't a usual reaction. The protest around the country scared the hell out of them as it could expand outside the universities' premises."

II

Time flew fast, and sneaked the final exams like a giant python shrinking the students' minds to the extent that everybody had only one thought—finish the semester. Most students had bought a bus or train ticket several days or even weeks before the exams. They preferred to leave as soon as they were done with the last test. Looking forward to heading back to their cities or going on holidays, everyone in the dormitory had their suitcase packed and ready.

In less than two weeks, almost everybody had already finished all their exams and wrapped up the year. I couldn't wait to take a break, get back home, and catch up with my family and friends. Farid and I had only one final exam to take care of and officially complete our second academic year.

Among the craziness of all those tests and exams, Cultural Units had been frequently asking students to support the nationwide protest upon finishing our final tests, either there or in other cities. The focus was mainly on the dormitory, as all students from different colleges could be updated from Tehran every day. That was the strategy from the beginning, so the summer holiday could not impact the plan too much.

It was the second week of July. I woke up a bit late and was not surprised that Farid was still sleeping as we had been studying till late the night before. Yawning, I knocked on his door.

"Wake up, buddy. We should be there before lunch."

A mumbling voice answered, "What time is it?"

Pushing the door open, I said, "It's almost half past ten. Abbas and Reza start at eleven. Come on, we're gonna be late."

I stood in front of his room, stared at him, and locked my hands behind my neck stretching backward just enough to relax my back muscles. Farid rubbed his eyes and tried the exact same thing before lazily getting out of bed.

We had a plan for a final review on our last exam with the folks in the dormitory. I gathered my stuff and threw them into my backpack while Farid walked out of his room and started to brew tea in a new flowery China teapot which Taban had bought for me a week before.

"No time to drink anything. We'll have something at the dorm with the other boys. Let's go! And don't forget your toothbrush. We're gonna sleep over tonight," I shouted from my room while searching for my thermodynamics book among the clutter of T-shirts, books, blankets, my half-open suitcase, shorts, pants, and several socks in different colours.

"The last one! Thermodynamics! Isn't it fabulous to finish the year with your most favourite course of all time, buddy? We'll be back home soon!" Farid yelled from his room and clapped his hands, yawning and gathering his things at the same time.

"Why are you bringing your tennis racket? We're gonna study today!" I chuckled, asking Farid curiously.

"This beauty is for tomorrow after our last exam. Amin has already booked a court near the uni. We'll catch up and play right after the exam." He chuckled and caressed his racket.

"Do you mean the day after or an hour after the exam? The day after tomorrow will be the demonstration. We'll be busy before our leave."

"I know, silly. I meant after the final exam. Tomorrow!"

The sun, like a giant boiling ball, showed no sign of mercy turning the entire city into a convection oven with its fan on. Walking for several minutes under the wide shadows from the tall, plain trees on both sides of the street, we eventually gave up and decided to take a cab. Luckily, it wasn't a busy day and we arrived at the dormitory almost on time.

We walked into the building, not expecting to see anyone. Almost half of the students had left the town and their rooms were empty. Most of the doors were locked on the first floor. We took the first staircase and went to the upper levels, where more sounds were coming out of the rooms. Passing door by door and glancing inside the open ones, we reached Abbas's room.

"Hi pals, how's it going here? Are we ready to rock and roll?" I shouted, entering the room.

Reza was lying on the ground and Abbas was near the window. Their roommates had finished their exams the day before and left. Books, notebooks, calculators, a half-empty tea mug, unwashed dishes, and a pair of jeans were scattered on the carpet all over the room. I murmured, "You nerds started without us?"

We all chuckled while Farid looked for a clean mug and tried to set up the electric kettle for making tea.

"Gentlemen, let's start with an example on entropy, page thirty-seven," Abbas yelled with his book in his hands, pushing a puffy pillow away with his foot. "It is so hot today!"

We managed to review a few questions during the next couple of hours. Reza was humming every other minute, and

I was breathing heavily. Abbas took off his T-shirt and threw it towards his bunk bed, but missed. "Bloody stuffy here," he whispered.

The window was fully open, but there was no sign of air circulation inside the room. Wiping the droplets of warm sweat from my head, I tried to remember the thermodynamics formulas and how to use them for resolving complicated problems.

"It'll be an open book exam, Nima. You don't need to memorize everything!" Reza said.

I laughed. "I know, mate. But this subject was always interesting to me. I loved it more than any other topic. Gibbs Energy! This is insane! Many scientists have been working to control aging. And it all comes back to Gibbs Energy! You might have a chance to stop getting old! Staying young forever! Eternal life!" The words came out of my mouth oddly louder than I anticipated.

Reza smiled. "Yes, yes, you talk about it non-stop. At least you got an A on the midterm test, and you'll certainly pass this tutorial with the top grade." He looked at my drafts to check the answers. "Well, that's correct. Oh, beautiful pen, Nima. Fancy one!" said Reza with childish excitement while he took my pen.

"It is a gift," I replied with a long pause.

Abbas turned his face and glanced at me. "A gift? This is gonna be interesting. Do we know *her*?" he asked with a grin and stared at Farid for an answer.

I replied, "Of course, you do! Now shut up and let's eat something. I'm starving!"

Farid burst out with a loud laughter and added, "Live forever! Young forever! Viva, Gibbs Theory!"

Still joking around, we headed out for a late lunch. The canteen wasn't busy, no queue, no humming noise, and the best part was—no waiting. Eating my overcooked chicken thighs with white rice, I asked the guys' feeling about the upcoming demonstration. Reza assured me again that they would certainly join the protest and he was hopeful about the outcome. Then we started to talk about our plans for the summer. Farid proposed renting a villa near the Caspian Sea and spending a few days there all together. I was looking at him, but my mind was somewhere else: *What's she going to do over the summer? Can we meet somewhere? Can she join us near the Caspian Sea? I don't want to miss this summer again.*

Something inside my brain was poking my nerves, manipulating my thoughts, and constantly bothering me. Something like being powerless, or maybe it was lack of freedom. I couldn't figure it out, but it had been bugging me for a long time.

"Pals, I'm gonna go call my parents. You continue with the next chapter, and I'll join you later," I said, bewildered, leaving my half-finished lunch tray in the return rack, and headed to the dormitory telephone centre.

As I walked away, Farid yelled, "Nima? Nima! Is everything alright?"

I replied, "Yes, I'll be back soon. You start without me." I spun around and took off at a slow jog.

The telephone centre was not far from the canteen, but I didn't enter the building. I used a public pay-phone adjacent to the west wall, which was for local calls inside the city. I dropped a coin and dialled while I tried to separate my wet T-shirt from my back.

"Hello?"

"Hi, Taban. It's Nima. How are you?"

"Hi, Nima. I'm doing well. Thanks. Yourself?"

"I'm well. Thanks. I'm in the dorm now, studying for tomorrow's exam with the folks. How's it going on your end? Ready for tomorrow? Last one!"

"Yeah, the last one to wrap up the second year."

"Listen, I'm just wondering if we could catch up?"

"Catching up? You mean now?! Is everything okay?"

"Yes. Yes. Everything is fine. I just want a quick catch-up. Whenever you are free."

"What about six o'clock? My place?"

"Awesome! I'll be there."

I hung up the phone, got goosebumps, and let out my breath. My legs shook a bit, but I managed to control myself. Standing near the telephone centre for a few moments, I inhaled a deep, warm breath and puffed it out with a loud noise. I rubbed my sweaty head with my right sticky hand several times. Looking at the half-constructed building on the horizon, I smiled and walked back to the dormitory, but not to Abbas's room. I thought I would pay a visit to Saber and ask if he had bought a ticket to Tehran. His plan was to leave the town after the demonstration. Farid and I would be joining him on the night train.

A couple of students were walking in the corridor and laughing loudly while talking about their summer holidays. Saber's room's door was open, and I overheard some familiar voices inside. Karim was chatting with Jalal while Saber was packing up his things. A half-full large suitcase was laid wide open on the floor and a jumble of folded clothes, books, and folders were scattered around it.

"Oh man, how did you manage to hoard all this shit? You need at least three suitcases! So, did you find a ticket on our train?" I asked Saber.

He sat on the ground, trying to push everything inside the already overstuffed suitcase. He smiled and replied, "Nope, not yet. All sold out. I'll leave with the late train at midnight. When is your exam? Tomorrow morning or afternoon?"

I took a seat near the window. "Yup. The last one. Tomorrow at ten o'clock."

Saber took the books and folders from the carpet and layered them in his suitcase. "Sounds good! So, we can meet after your final exam. Let's have lunch together and finalize our plan for the demonstration. We want to go to the kebab restaurant near Azad Park around twelve-thirty. Is that okay for you and Farid?"

"Works for me, since that's right after my exam! But Farid has a plan to play tennis with Amin afterward."

Karim took off his shirt and laid on the bed. Trying to fit a pillow under his back, he murmured, "This will be my bed from tomorrow. Not bad!"

I chuckled. "What do you mean? Are you moving into this room?"

"Unfortunately, yes!" Jalal shouted from the other side of the bed. "I couldn't find anyone else to room with. Everybody has gone and I didn't want dormitory management to send a stranger to my room!"

We all laughed. Saber had almost taken care of all the packing. He didn't zip the luggage, just pushed it against the wall.

"So, any news from anywhere?" I asked, glancing at the blazing horizon from the open window.

Jalal sighed. "We are so hopeful about the demonstration. Our prediction is a massive show up here. Tehran University also expects a large crowd there, too."

We talked a bit longer and then I went back to Abbas's room. The guys were resting, scattered around the room.

"What took you so long?" Farid asked. "Where have you been?"

I told him about the protest plan and laid down on the floor carpet. "When do we start again?" I asked Abbas.

He was trying to take a nap. "Four or maybe five," he replied and yawned.

"I'll knock off at about half past five and come back later," I whispered.

Farid stretched his neck to his right side and stared at me. "What? Where are you going, mate? We don't have that much time. We'll be lucky if we finish the book by midnight. We're behind our schedule."

I glanced at the other guys to make sure their eyes were still closed, then I turned to Farid and mouthed, "I'm going to see *Taban*."

He smirked and mouthed back, "*Good* for *you*."

III

Humming heatwave floating around with feeble waft resulted in a sizzling afternoon. I bought a pack of vanilla ice cream from a small shop close to Taban's place and walked fast to reach there before it melted into runny cream. When I arrived, Taban's fully open book, some sticky notes, a couple of pens, and her brand-new Casio engineering calculator were laid on the left end of her small coffee table. A bunch of white roses rested in a translucent crystal vase, half filled with clean water, in the middle of the table. Taban wore a white top with a dark blue skirt that reached her knees without any socks.

"Oh, you almost finished the book. Lucky you! We boys are just halfway through. Four more chapters to go."

"Come on, Nima. You're on top of this course! You got the best score on the midterm."

Her glowing eyes were like pure crystal that I could see myself drowning in deeply. The self-confidence in her gaze combined with her tender gestures always made my heart beat faster. She had dared to break apart the stupid rules for women and the superstitious traditions in such a religious society. Getting in touch with boys and hanging around was not acceptable behaviour in the fanatic communities, but she was not afraid at all to bite the forbidden apple and mock the judging eyes.

"This is my theory: all of us, our generation, are sick! We are mentally sick! Strict, suffocating religious rules will gradually

189

turn us into either dormant psychos or mental zombies," I told Taban while finishing my ice cream, leaning forward and putting the empty plate on the coffee table.

She attentively replied, "I understand. I'm not a psychologist, but don't you reckon this point of view is harsh? Not all of us are mentally sick. Some of us may still have a chance." She smiled.

"I hope so," I said, and we both chuckled.

"What are your plans for the first week of August?" she asked me out of the blue.

"What?" I took a tissue and wiped the sticky sweetness on my lips.

"I'm asking about your plans. Are you free in August?"

"I think so. Why?"

"I'd like to invite you to my city. My bestie is getting married and I'm wondering if you'd like to be my plus one."

"What?!" I almost shouted. My jaw dropped for a couple of seconds, and my gaze were pinned towards her eyes.

"I told her about you, and she gladly invited you." She said it tenderly and then, for a split of a second, caressed my arm.

"Taban, um… I don't know what to say." I was burning from inside. Trying to avoid shaking, I said, "Um… This is unexpectedly pleasant and interesting. Honestly, I wanted to somehow see you over the summer. This is beyond my expectations!"

"Excellent! So, I'll tell her you'll join us."

"What about your parents?" I muttered.

"What about them? They know about you."

I shifted a bit and adjusted my back against the sofa, glancing at the white roses for a few moments wordlessly. A feeling of warm comfort mixed with scorching sexual desire and self-control was messing with my brain. I couldn't focus or properly articulate what I wanted to say. It was a sensational moment for me. I had not expected it at all. *It is not only me.*

She feels so close to me that she already talked about me with her parents and bestie, I thought to myself while she walked to the kitchen. Trying to grasp what had just happened, I followed her. She was washing fresh summer fruits.

"What are you doing? No need. I'm gonna go soon. The guys are waiting for me at the dorm," I said, but did not mean it. I sincerely wanted to stay with her, more.

She took a colourful dish towel and dried two big peaches, then put them on a plate. "Can't you stay a bit more? We can study together if you are nervous about the exam?"

Leaning back against the kitchen wall, I answered, "Seriously? Is that fine with you? But what about the guys? They are waiting for me."

Adding a green apple, a couple of blushing apricots, and a handful of dark red cherries to the same plate, she replied, "Of course, it is okay. They won't be worried. But they will talk behind your back, since Farid knows you are with me."

I laughed. "Farid's mouth is locked. He won't tell them. But so what? Let him tell them!" I chuckled and took the fruit dish and put it on the coffee table.

She walked out with two cups of tea and sat near me on the sofa. Her knee accidentally touched my leg while she was trying to serve me the tea. Again, came the burning flame flared up inside my whole body. Her wavy black hair silently danced in front of my eyes. Soaking in her soft floral smell, I tried to take a deep breath. She blushed and stared at me without saying anything. I shivered. My heart beat faster. Gazing at each other, I slowly moved my shaking hand and touched her fingers that were resting on her thigh. I looked at her hand and smoothly caressed her bright red shiny nails. She did not move at all. Gently, I turned my upper body toward her and held both of her hands. They were so soft and smooth. I could feel her heartbeats, as I sensed mine, too. Her thick ruby lips started to tremble. Her huge black eyes were wide open and led me deep through her mind, where a silvery voice invited me to unleash my desire and fly into her sophisticated world. Leaning closer to her glowing face, I hovered in the warm, smooth heat radiating from her body. My palms began to sweat. Staring into the deep ocean of her eyes, I felt her hands move behind my neck as I melted within her breath drifting on my face. Closing my eyes, I put my hands on both sides of her neck, tenderly caressed her soft skin, and gently laid my lips on hers.

IV

It was late when I kissed Taban goodbye and left her apartment. Whispering folklore songs and picturing Taban in my arms, I strolled all the way back to the dormitory. Luckily, the security man was not in his cabin and the main entrance to the building was open. *They might be still awake,* I thought when I glanced at a narrow band of white light under the door. Pushing the door as quietly as possible, I sneaked into the room. Abbas was lying down half-naked near the open window, drinking tea from a big mug and reading a journal. Reza was on his back on the lower bunk bed, while Farid rested on the upper one, listening to music with his headphones in his ears.

"You haven't slept yet!" I said quietly.

Abbas laughed. "Where the hell have you been? I'm gonna take the upper bed. You'll sleep there." He pointed to the lower one opposite Reza.

Farid smiled and winked at me. "Okay dokey. He's back! Time to sleep. Turn off the light, please, and keep the window open. I'm sweating like a pig!"

Abbas left the mug near the window and jumped into the upper bed while I tried to find my book. "Where is my stuff?"

"Under the bed. Now, wrap it up and get to bed," Abbas answered.

I bent to see under the bed. Stretching my arm, I dragged some items out. There was my book, with my pen on top of it. Looking at the sparkling reflection of the lamp bulb on my pen, I smiled, put the book in my backpack, and kept the pen in my hand. I turned off the lamp and laid on the lower bunk bed. Staring at the pen under the feeble moonlight from the window, I dreamt about the future, visualizing Taban and myself together near a sandy beach far from crowded cities. We were walking on a breathtaking green land, shoulder to shoulder, hand in hand. Looking around, we walked faster and smoothly took off from the ground. We were freely flying over turquoise islands and looking at dolphins dancing in the shiny azure ocean.

Looking at her dancing wavy black hair, I said, "Taban, let's stay here. This place is wonderful."

We landed on a vast, golden, sandy beach. Stepping on the powdery tracks, my feet got warmer and warmer. I held her hands tight and gazed into her exuberant, ocean-hued eyes. She leaned towards me and rested her head on my right shoulder. My hands started sweating and I felt her warm breath inside my chest. Suddenly, I saw over her shoulder a group of men in dark army clothes approaching us. They had long beards and were wearing militia outfits. Some of them had transceivers in their hands, while others had metal batons or black whips made of electrical cables. I was choking. My whole body began to shiver in fear. I dragged Taban behind my back, but my legs were not able to hold my weight. I could neither move nor open my mouth. The sun dissolved inside a giant grey cloud. Everything was dark now and my body was soaked in stinky sweat. Looking around, I could not see Taban anymore. I had lost her. The men with batons were yelling and swearing. One of them ran towards me with a black gun in his hand. Trying to cry for help, I found myself on my knees in front of him. He spat and shouted on me furiously. My head was down. I could not understand him as he was yelling in a different language. I raised my head inch by inch and looked at a terrifying prayer bump on his forehead. He was Mr. Haji from the Islamic Council. He did not say anything, pointed his gun at my face, and pulled the trigger. Next, I saw myself soaked in blood, and then the sun came out of the grey clouds. It was not the sun, though. It was a gigantic prayer bump on a forehead.

I woke up, shivering, sweating, and breathless. Struggling to sit up and take a deep breath, I could still hear the men shouting.

"What's happening? What's that noise?" Reza asked with a sleepy voice.

The noise came from inside the building, and it was getting louder and louder.

"Is there a fight out there?" asked Abbas, trying to jump down from the upper bed.

The clattering noises got closer to us, and clearer. It was the sound of breaking glass, cracking doors, and shouts for help. I was still shivering. Abbas reached to turn on the light, but before he could, someone kicked the door open. The door fell from its hinges and hung crooked on the bottom side.

The light from the hallway hit my eyes and I saw two bulky bodies with black batons in hand storming inside the room. They were entirely in black, wearing face masks, yelling, and breaking everything in their way, swearing repeatedly. "Get the fuck out of here, now!"

I was so terrified that could not say a word. One of them punched Abbas in his stomach and hit him on the shoulder with the baton. I was appalled and tried to assist him, but another man grabbed my neck and shoved me to the bed mattress. He beat me on the back with the baton and kicked my left leg with his army boot. Pain radiated from my back.

I shouted for help, trying desperately to get out of the room. They were destroying everything and howling, "Get lost! All of you, get out now!"

Protecting my head with both of my hands, I struggled to crawl to the door so I could reach the hallway, but I was unable to move. Rubbing my left leg to reduce the pain, I heard Farid crying for help. I glanced back where the other man punched Farid in the face. Farid went silent. I turned trying to stand up while Farid's tennis racket near the bed caught my eyes. I gathered all my energy, grabbed the racket tightly with both hands, moving towards Farid's bed, and slammed the man on the back of his head with the edge of the racket. He screamed, turned back to me like a giant, wounded bull and forcefully put his right hand on my face, pushing my head. I staggered and lost my balance as I hopelessly tried to grab and hold on to something, anything, but he kicked my back and I fell near the door. I tried to drag myself out of the room, but he threw a tea mug towards me. It hit the wall right in front of my face and I felt broken ceramics shattered and pierced my eyes. I screamed in pain and put my hands on my face. The massive burning pain in my right eye was unbearable.

Reza begged for help on the other side of the room. I kept my palm on my right eye, looked back, and vaguely saw the shadow of someone hitting Abbas and Farid with a baton. I shouted, "Leave them alone! What do you want from us? Leave them alone!"

The raging man stopped, and Abbas ran out of his reach, towards me. He took my arm, and we dragged ourselves to the corridor. We looked back to the room and yelled, "Reza, Farid, run!"

Barely standing on my feet in the hallway, my hand over my right eye, I could see the same fighting situation happening in other rooms. Black men in masks were hitting students and breaking everything. All of a sudden, a throttling sound followed by a greyish plume filled the entire corridor. A loud voice echoed in the corridor, someone shouting in fear, "Tear gas! Tear gas!"

Abbas screamed, "Nima, run! Let's get out of here."

Keeping my hand over my right eye, I said, "I can't fucking run. I can't move my left leg, and…" I stammered, "and… my right eye, my eye is burning."

Abbas hurriedly pushed me forward. "Yes, you can move your leg! Come on, just follow me!"

I hobbled, trying not to fall down as my eyes filled with tears or sweat or blood. Whatever it was, I felt the burning wave inside my skull. I focused on holding my breath, trying to avoid inhaling the sharp, tangy cloud around us. In addition to my eyes, I sensed my throat burning, too. "Abbas, let's go to the toilet. We can run water over our heads till the cloud disappears in the hallway."

Abbas didn't say anything, pushed me towards the wall. I laid back there for a few seconds. The billowing thick cloud was everywhere, flooding around us, and we could not get away from it. "There, let's go! Fast!" Abbas shouted and dragged me to the toilet room. He kicked the door with his leg, led me inside, and slammed the door behind us.

My eyes were filled with tears and pain. I could neither stop crying nor open my right eye. Limping in pain, I sat down on the floor, shocked by the cold tiles. I kept my eyes closed, both of them, and for no reason, just for a few seconds, scenes from my first day of the university appeared in my fearful darkness like a mirage.

Some moments later, Abbas turned on the tap water. "Come here, Nima. Put your head under the water," he said breathlessly.

I blindly chased the sound of water and attempted to find my way with the tips of my numbed fingers.

Abbas took my hand. "Here, stand here." He helped me bend my back and led my head to the running water.

My head was on the verge of exploding. An invisible force pounded my skull from the inside. After a few moments, I was able to control my hands and lightly ran the warm water on my eyes. "Shit. That burns." I slowly opened my left eye and put my lips near the tip of the pull-out spray, trying to bear the pain. It was difficult to drink as my throat was itchy and water seemed incapable of washing the deep-seated bitter dryness.

Abbas opened the window and stayed near me.

"Let me see your eye." He whispered coarsely, held on to my neck as he examined my eye.

"What the fuck just happened? Who are they?" I asked, not expecting an answer while we were fearfully lingering in the toilet room.

"Listen!" Abbas said, trying to get up. "No more shouting. It is quiet out."

"Have they gone?"

"Probably yes. Let me check," said Abbas, headed to the door.

He glanced at me and then worriedly pushed the door. There was still a thin layer of pungent grey cloud in the corridor, so he quickly shut the door again.

"I reckon they've gone. Couldn't see anything," he muttered, walking back and putting his head under the water again. "I don't feel well," Abbas muffled, and threw up on the floor before he could say anything else.

I stood up and tried to help him with my left hand. "Abbas, are you okay?" I asked, leading him to the window.

"I'm fine. Let's see if we can get out," he whispered.

He went to the door and into the hallway, leaving me behind in the toilet room. A few minutes later, Abbas peered out again and said, "I think it is safe now. Let's go."

As we sneaked out of the toilet, I heard weak, vague muttering from all over the corridor. I tried to see what was going on, but I still could not open my right eye. Inside, the rooms were dim, and it was difficult to see with my half-open left eye.

"They destroyed everything," Abbas said, startled.

Holding my hand to the hallway wall, I limped to Abbas's room while glimpsing around where students were helping each other.

Abbas dragged his hand along the wall and found the lamp switch. He clicked it up and down, and up and down, but it did not work. "They broke all lamps, too," he said.

The fluorescent lights in the hallway were still on and made the inside of the room a bit visible. It took a few seconds for my left eye to adjust to the darkness.

"Be careful. There are broken glasses everywhere," Abbas said feebly, and that was the moment I realized I had bare feet and wearing wet underwear.

"Farid and Reza aren't here. Let's find our clothes and get the hell of here," Abbas said while he was cautiously crawling through the smashed room. I breathed heavily, remembering that I had left my clothes under the bed. I sat down on the floor and crawled to the bed I had been sleeping in. It was pitch black under the bed, so I straightened my arm, struggling to find my stuff without looking. I touched a pair of pants, dragged them out, and turned to the side to see them in the hallway light. Bending again, I pushed more and patted the ground carefully. My hand touched something like a rubbery piece of pipe. I pulled it out. It was Farid's tennis racket and I instantly recalled how I had hit the man with it.

"Farid, Farid!" I shouted, struggling to move.

Abbas turned back and walked towards me. "What? Farid what?"

I shivered. "Look at his bed. See if Farid is on his bed. Come on."

Abbas startled and worriedly moved back to the bunk bed and stepped onto the side ladder to check on the upper section. "Oh, my God. Farid! Farid!" Abbas shouted, trying to move Farid with his right hand. "Can you hear me?" screamed Abbas a couple of times. A sob escaped him.

I dragged myself closer and tried to see his bed.

Abbas moved away, leaving the room. He stood in the corridor, crying and shouting, "Help! Help, please! Someone, help us."

I saw Farid on his bed, motionless. His face was still wet with blood. I stepped back and shouted, too, my entire body trembling. "Help! Help! Someone call an ambulance." I tried to walk out of the room, but my right eye burned, and the sharp pain penetrated my head. I stopped and held my head with both hands. I struggled to hold on to the wall, and the last thing I remembered was Abbas's voice begging for help.

CHAPTER 11

I

woke up, a bit dizzy and confused. My neck was sore, but my headache was gone. It took more than a few seconds for my vision to adjust to the darkness of the room. There was just enough light to follow a long hose from a plastic serum cylinder above my head down to my right hand. A few people were talking somewhere outside of the room where I was lying, and I occasionally heard random footsteps of people coming or going.

Struggling to get out of the squeaky bed, I suffered an unbearable pain in my spine as I tried to move, and I realized my left leg was in a temporary cast, something like a splint.

"Is anyone here?" The words came out of my mouth weaker than expected. "Hello? Can anyone hear me?" I looked around again. It was like a temporary compartment segregated from other areas with a thick curtain. The smell of alcohol mixed with other disinfectants was all over the place. I could see feeble fluorescent lighting from outside of the enclosure. *Where am I? What is this place?* I was about to attempt to get out of bed one more time, when the curtain was pulled aside and a skinny man in a white robe with a stereoscope around his neck walked in.

"You are awake. How are you feeling?"

"Where am I, doctor? What happened?" I asked quite shakily, struggling to sit up.

"Relax. Don't move. Stay in your current position, alright? Do you understand me?"

"Yes, doctor. Where am I?"

"You are in Rezvan Hospital, the emergency section."

"How did I get here? Where are my friends?"

"Calm down. You cannot move. I'll repeat it again: you must not move. We're very busy tonight. Something has happened at the university dormitory. An ambulance brought you here. Maybe your friends are around, but I don't know for sure."

"I have to see them. Doctor, please."

"Keep calm. I'll check if anyone's outside. Now, answer my questions. What's your name?"

"My name? Nima."

"How old are you?"

"Twenty."

"Where are you from?"

"Tehran."

"What are you doing in Mashhad?"

"Sorry? What?"

"Why are you here? Why are you in Mashhad? Can you remember?"

"Oh, doctor, my memory is fine. I'm a student here at the Engineering College."

"Very good. Do you have anyone here?"

"My uncles and aunties."

"Very good. Do you have their phone numbers?"

"I wrote all the numbers in my phonebook. I can't recall them."

"That's enough for now."

"Doctor! My friends. I have to see them. Are they okay?"

"Some students are outside. I'll tell them you are awake."

"Thanks."

"No problem. Now I'm going to take a blood sample. Do you know your blood type?"

"No, I'm not sure."

"That's fine, I'll check it anyway." He paused. "I'll inject another painkiller in your serum."

He tore the wrapper off a syringe pack, took my left hand to find a vein, and jabbed the tip of the needle in my forearm. Dark blood filled the small syringe's bottle in seconds. He wrote something on it, injected a painkiller in the serum, and headed out.

The curtain was left open a bit, and I could see a tiny portion of the outside through the gap. A few minutes later, I felt dizzy like my head had gained weight pushing my eyes. I could still hear some voices and feel flickers of shadows flying around, chunky black silhouettes, something like deep dark hallows with sparkling spots around them. I tried to catch them, one by one. Stretching my hands towards the dazzling shadows, I lightly pulled myself out of the bed, and floated into an infinite void space. The black silhouettes disappeared, while glittering, shiny green, red, and turquoise auroras on the horizon waved at me. My eyes widened; it was breathtaking. I was blessed with power and eternity. Sensational colourful waves danced all over the sky, and I was flying among them. Looking down, I saw white horses galloping across an enormous, golden colza farm. It seemed they were chasing the auroras on the horizon. I flew lower, skimming along the top of the delicate tiny flowers and found myself among the horses. We were moving fast towards the skyline where the aurora was turning into a huge golden and white hallow, like a giant blazing sun. The closer we got, the faster we grew, bigger and bigger. The light grew, too, vaster and vaster. It was all light. I was the sun. I was the light. The light... The light...

II

Daylight from the grimy windows made the room bright. Looking around, I saw other beds in the room, maybe two, maybe three. I couldn't scan all the corners very well, but I realized that I was in a normal room in the hospital, not the emergency section.

"Nima! How are you feeling?"

I turned to the familiar voice and there she was, Taban, standing near the bed. Her trembling wet eyes were swollen in a red shadow of sorrow.

"Taban?"

"How are you?"

"I don't know. Where am I?"

"Rezvan Hospital."

"Why are you here?"

"I came as soon as I heard what happened. I couldn't believe it, no one could."

"Where are the others?"

"You shouldn't talk too much. Save your energy. Relax. I must call the doctor. Wait." She wiped her eyes and hurriedly left the room.

Moving a bit to my right side, I turned my head and glanced around. A few people were in the room near other beds, but I couldn't recognize them. Minutes later, Taban and a doctor entered the room. He wasn't the doctor I had met in the emergency section. He was a bit older with a grey goatee. A tall nurse was following them with a black clipboard in her hand.

"How are you feeling, young man?" said the doctor with a smile.

"I'm fine."

"Any pain?"

"No."

"Good, good. You had an urgent operation on your right eye last night. We washed and took all external particles out. I'm now going to examine it. Alright?"

I did not answer. Only at that moment, I felt a bandage on my right eye. I glanced at Taban with my left eye. I wanted to grab her hands, but I could not. She was crying and turned her face away as soon as she caught my glimpse. "It may hurt a bit, but that's normal," the doctor whispered while he took off the layers of bandage like peeling an onion. I did not feel anything, no pain, no burning, no itchiness. He pointed a medical penlight into my right eye. He murmured a few words, and the nurse near him came closer, poured a couple of droplets into my eye, and smoothly layered a new, sterile bandage on the same place. The doctor injected something into my serum and said, "Very well. Let me know if you feel pain and I'll give you another painkiller. Now, it is better to rest, young man."

"Doctor! What's happening? My eyes?"

"Don't worry. Now just rest." He didn't explain anything more, just showed a quick smile and then left the room.

Taban was standing near me with shimmering, red, swollen eyes, clutching a crumbled tissue in her hand. She leaned towards the bed, warmly grabbed my hand with her right hand and put her left hand on my head, bent a bit, and softly asked, "Nima, do you know your aunt's phone number? The hospital must inform your family."

"I can't remember my aunt's number, but I know my parents'. I don't want to make them nervous."

"You must tell them." She gazed at me, holding my hand like we have been together since we born. "The number please. I'll call them."

I became lightheaded again, but managed to mutter the phone number before my eyelids covered my eyes like a feathery blanket.

"You sleep now," Taban said and kissed my forehead. "I'll let them know. They could call your aunt or uncle here..." I felt warm, did not hear the last words, and had fallen asleep.

I wasn't sure how long I'd been sleeping. The inside of the room was still bright with feeble sunlight when I opened my left eye. Some people were talking quietly in the room near the other beds. I didn't turn my head to see them. My back ached, and I had to go to the toilet. Trying to sit up on my bed, I heard someone yell, "Hey, Nima! You are up. How are you, buddy?" Before I could turn to the direction of the voice, Amin walked in front of me.

"What do you want, buddy? You shouldn't move. Wait." Amin darted out without waiting to hear my answer. In a few minutes, he came back with the same doctor and nurse.

"I need to go to the restroom." The words came out coarsely, scratching my throat.

The doctor glanced at my serum. "No problem. We'll bring you a urine catheter. Don't move."

Another nurse in a purple uniform came with an opaque catheter and asked Amin to leave. He hid the bed from the view of others with a portable stand drape and set up the urine catheter between my legs. "That should work. I'll wait behind the curtain. Buzz me when you finish," the nurse told me, and stood behind the drape. I tried to hold the container with my hand and adjust my butt. I could hear that the catheter was filling. When I was done, I glanced over at the drape and called the nurse. He came near me, took out the catheter, pulled the sheet back over my legs, and left without taking the portable curtain.

A few minutes later Amin, Taban, and my younger aunt and uncle showed up. My aunt was wiping her face with a bunch of tissues, trying not to cry in front of me. She stood on the left side of the bed and said, "Don't worry. We are here."

I smiled. "Thanks."

My uncle added, "Your dad and mom are on their way. They took the first flight and should be here by tonight. I'll go pick them up from the airport."

I breathed in, paused, and exhaled easily. After some minutes, my aunt and uncle left the room, leaving Amin and Taban standing near me.

Taban came closer and cupped my forehead inside her delicate hand. It was warm and soft like a pillow. I looked at her and smiled, then asked Amin, "What the hell happened?"

"No one has a freaking clue. Rumour has it, the raid was most probably planned by the Ministry of Intelligence. Saber told me just couple of minutes ago."

"How is Saber? Where is he now?"

"He's fine. He was released from the hospital last night."

"What about Farid? Where is he? Is he okay?"

Amin did not say anything. I stretched my neck and glanced at Taban. She walked away and turned back to the window, her shaky hands on her face. I gathered all my power and said, "Where is Farid?"

"Um, he's not fine. Nima, listen. Um, he's in a coma," Amin muttered.

Something pressed against my throat, and I endured a heavy pressure on my chest. For some moments, I was unable to breathe, talk, or even think. I could not believe it. My left eye filled with tears. "Where is he?"

Amin shook his head and bit his lips. He quickly wiped his own tears with the back of his hand. "Nima, you need rest. He is here. I think they brought him out of the ICU and transferred him to a private room. His father flew in early this morning."

Trying to breathe, I heard another doctor talking with my aunt near the bed. Holding an x-ray result in his hand, the new doctor came closer and asked me to move my back to the side. I did so, and I felt him unfasten something from my spine. A minute later, he said, "All good. I've just removed the guard vest from your back. Fortunately, you had no spinal damage. That's great news. You are so lucky. Be careful for a few days. Avoid sudden movement. I'll give you further instructions later..."

I did not hear anything more. Suspended in a deep, dark sorrow, I closed my eye. The last thing I wanted was to be awake.

III

One week passed with frequent dizziness, random hallucinations, sporadic pain, and non-stop nightmares. It was the most painful, grief-stricken time of my life, full of the gloomiest memories that will never fade away.

Farid did not make it. He died while I was still in the hospital. His doctor reported the cause of death as internal bleeding and brain injury, but the detailed report was never issued. Agents from the Ministry of Intelligence were in every corner of the hospital. They were monitoring the staff and altering documents that were related to that night. Less than a day after Farid's death, the city police chief officially closed the case. They recorded the fatality as the result of a fight, claiming Farid had been hit on his skull by a pipe.

Saber told me later that the media did not cover anything but some minor fake information. They called it "Night of Unrest at the Dormitory." All mass media were completely under government control—TV, radio, newspapers. There was no other platform to reveal the real tragedy of how Farid had been killed by unknown savages while sleeping in his bed. The newspapers only published a short, altered, misleading headline: "Unfortunate Isolated Accident."

Farid's father was called to the Ministry of Intelligence office in Mashhad a day after Farid's death. He told me later that they threatened to put him behind bars, expel his daughter from ever pursuing education, and plant a shameful sexual scandal all over the news. He didn't explain in further detail, and I did not ask more. His shuddering voice, a silent scream of self-hatred, misery, and despair, pounded in my head for years after that conversation.

Farid's father wasn't the only person who was brutally menaced by the regime. All of us were approached by unknown agents and horrifically threatened. Each of us was called and bullied in a different way, but with a common theme—*our families*. I received several short visits at the hospital on different nights. There had not been enough light to remember their faces, or maybe I just hadn't had enough energy inside me to look at them, but I never forgot their sickening voices.

I was released from the hospital three days after Farid's death. Although my father insisted on staying at my aunt's home, I preferred to head back to my apartment. My parents, elder uncle, Taban, and Amin all came to the hospital to help bring me back. Apparently, my parents had already met Taban.

Trying to put on my shoes, I looked at Taban. "You should've gone back home to your city a week ago. I don't know what to say."

Taban was standing near the window, looking out. "How could I?"

It was around noon when we arrived at my place. Amin helped me to walk downstairs while Taban opened the door. Before I went into the apartment, my father asked me, "Nima, are you okay? Do you need anything for now?"

"Thanks. I'm fine, Dad. You need rest, too."

My parents went to my aunt's place and asked us to join them for dinner. Entering the apartment, my eye fixed on Farid's room. The door was half open. I stared in. It was empty. I did not ask anything. Holding myself together, I sat on the sofa in front of the TV. Taban leaned against the wall near my room. She stared at me without saying anything.

Amin approached me. "Farid's dad took some of the items and the rest went to charity. He thought it was better that way."

My face was cold, my hands shook, and my eye fixed on the dusty TV frame. I pressed my lips tightly together and did not respond. I didn't know what to say, and moreover, I did not want to think about it. *Farid was here one week ago, talking, walking, breathing, pouring tea, watching TV.* His voice was still in my head, *"I can't wait for the summer holiday. We need to chill out. Soon we will go back home! Isn't it awesome?"* I turned back to Taban, then glanced at Amin and stared at the empty room. *He never made it. He's gone, forever.*

Taban brought over a glass of water and cautiously placed it in my hand. She sat near me, keeping still while she held my hands and glanced at Amin. Her gleaming eyes were all wet like a deep lake. She could not hide her tears. "We are all grieving; these are moments of unbearable suffering. You need rest. Stress is the worst thing for you now. Your doctor said you have another operation soon and insisted on enough rest," Taban said. She turned her face to the other side and wiped her tears.

I sipped the water and let the cold flow move against my dry throat. I gently placed the glass on the table, raised my right hand, and touched the bandage over my eye. Clenching my left fist, I witnessed my sorrow gave way to anger and hatred, then changed back to suffering and suppression. It was like a mental firestorm, stuck inside me and I had no power to push it away. Glancing at Taban, I whispered, "Thank you."

She smoothly kissed me without saying a word.

I looked at her. "It is what it is. We must accept reality. The more I think about everything in my life, the more I believe that so-called God does not exist. Even if we fool ourselves and hope it exists, it certainly would be nothing but a useless dummy."

Taban and Amin shared a glance with no comments or reply.

Amin was about to say something, but the doorbell rang. "Who is it?" I asked.

Amin opened the door, and it was Saber, who limped in. His left arm was in a white cast that hung from his shoulder. He'd been staying at Amin's house since he had been released from the hospital. "So, did you talk with him again?" Amin asked Saber while he made tea in the kitchen.

Saber sat on a chair near Farid's room. He glanced inside briefly. "No, I did not. I put myself in his place."

"What's happening? Talk to whom?" I asked.

"We are chasing the dorm attack. I talked once with Farid's dad and asked him to file a lawsuit against the university. But as you are aware, he's been threatened several times. He is worried about his daughter now."

"I understand."

"We went to the central police station and officially reported what happened, but it stopped there. It is summer holiday and universities in other cities are closed, so we can't get more support from them either."

"They knew exactly what they were doing. What about Mr. Mohseni? Can he speak out and let people know what happened?"

"He can't publish anything. The government cancelled the NGO's license a couple of weeks ago. Media are under heavy censorship now. They altered everything."

"I still remember what he said in his seminar: the time of guns and violence had long gone, and we must learn how to resolve our differences with talking." I smirked so bitterly that my throat soared. "Where is he now? Where is he?" I cleared my throat. "The Ministry of Intelligence knew about the demonstration and raided the dorms to scare us, didn't they? What was the outcome of the protest in other cities? Nothing!"

Saber shook his head. Turning back, he gazed inside Farid's room and burst into tears. Amin came out of the kitchen with a tray of teacups. He quickly placed it on the coffee table and sat near Saber.

I asked, "Is it worth it? Look. Look at that room. It was full of life last week. Is it worth it?" I tried to stand up, but felt my head was about to blast away. A sharp pain moved from my back, up my neck like a sudden strike of whiplash.

No one said anything. We just stared at each other. I saw tears on Saber's face, I saw tears in Amin's eyes, and I saw tears on Taban's cheeks.

IV

The next day, I visited the eye clinic for the final check-up before my second surgery. It was early in the morning, but there was no sign of a refreshing breeze. I gave my sunglasses to my father and headed to the clinic entrance with Taban. My father stayed with Amin outside the building, near a narrow semi-garden area covered by yellowish grasses and scattered bunches of dried flowers. He waved his hand towards me while he was trying to dodge the sunlight within the slim shadow of the hospital's wall. He lit up his third or fourth or fifth cigarette of the day and turned his face towards the lawn.

Entering the waiting room, Taban sat on a free chair on the corner of the salon, and I walked into the examination room straightaway. A young nurse with a few wrinkles around her eyes and awkward makeup on her face asked me to lie on a medical armchair in the room. A couple minutes later, the doctor came in and started normal tests on my eye, checking pressure, dryness, nerves, and so on. "This is good. You are ready for the operation as we planned," the doctor confirmed while he switched off some buttons on the seat sideboard and the sleepy nurse put a new bandage on my eye.

I asked, "Doctor? Do I have any chance of getting my eyesight back?"

He pushed his chair away, stood up, and looked at me. A few seconds later, he grabbed the bandage from the nurse and

211

slowly put it on my eye, then fastened it with something like a headband behind my head. "Of course, young man. We do our best. It depends on how the nerves respond. You will get your vision back. Don't worry at all."

Taban was still in the waiting hall when I left the examination room. "That was quick! What did the doctor say?" Her voice calmed me down, dissipating the gloomy thoughts from my head. I felt so close to her. It was like we knew each other since we were born. Everything was different when she was with me.

I smiled. "Everything is going to be alright. The doctor confirmed that I'm ready for the second operation."

On our way out, I saw Amin pacing behind his car and talking on his mobile phone.

"Who is he talking to?" I asked my father, who was still smoking a bit farther away from Amin's car. He didn't know and instead asked me about my eye. I explained what the doctor had told me, then waited near Amin's car till he finished his conversation. A heat wave bounced from the surface of the car and slapped me in my face. I wiped my forehead with the back of my hand and yelled at Amin to open the car's door. He hung up the phone and moved towards us with a wrinkled forehead and clinching mouth.

"Is everything okay?" Taban asked.

"That was Saber," answered Amin quietly while he unlocked the car doors.

"And?" was my question.

Amin got into the car and turned on the engine. It was like a dry sauna inside the car. He ran the AC and put the fan on maximum power. I chose the back seat with Taban and my father sat in the front. Amin cleared his throat and muttered, "They expelled Saber from the university."

Two days after, Saber left the city. I had the second operation on my eye on the same day and could not accompany him to the train station. While I walked to the surgery room, I thought about what would have happened if we could turn time back two weeks, *only two bloody weeks.*

Lying on the leathery medical armchair, I shook my head unintentionally.

"Please don't move!" the doctor said as he fixed an eye holder hook into my right eye. Pouring in some eye drops, he explained the procedure for the second time, "It's going to take a couple of minutes for..." I did not hear him at all. My mind was somewhere else, far from that room, far from that city, far from that country. I was dreaming about a place free of prayer bumps on foreheads; a place where I could hold Taban's hand tight, and she could walk without a dark black cover on her head; a place with one common entrance for boys and girls; a place where no one was slaughtered in their own bed while dreaming about summer holidays; a place where I could breathe.

I did not go back to the university the next semester, or the term after, or even in the succeeding years. I began attending psychotherapy sessions to somehow heal the gravest wound of my life. It never worked, even when we left Iran forever, Taban and I. Whatever happened had happened. No one could undo what occurred that blistering summer.

"There are always inevitable instances in our life that change everything. No matter how powerful, cautious, or diligent we are, it isn't up to us to decide. Once that very moment arrives, it will diverge our life and alter our destiny forever." I murmured close to Taban's ears many years later. Years have passed since that gloomy summer, many years. But every time I see myself in a mirror, I remember it. I gently touch the dark blue guard over my right eye, fix it behind my head, and remember every single moment of the summer that changed my life.